Amazon River Vets

Romance straight out of the rain forest...

Sisters and vets Maria and Celine Dias's beloved animal sanctuary is in jeopardy. Their brother ran off with the wife of their biggest donor, and now their funding has been pulled! If they can't find financial support, then the charity that's been in their family for generations will have to close its doors.

The clinic has also been an emotional sanctuary for the sisters. When they've been at their lowest, it's been the one constant in both of their lives other than each other. But will it still be there now that they are about to experience the biggest highs of their lives?

Read Maria and Rafael's story in
The Vet's Convenient Bride

Discover Celine and Darius's story in
The Secret She Kept from Dr. Delgado

Both available now!

Dear Reader,

Welcome to book two of the Amazon River Vets duet, *The Secret She Kept from Dr. Delgado*. I'm especially excited to introduce you to the Dias sisters, Maria and Celine, who both aspire to make the world a better place through what they do with their animal charity.

This story is about Celine Dias, the younger Dias sister, and her estranged husband, Darius Delgado, who vanished from her life five years ago.

I adore Celine and Darius's story so much that it took me less than a month to write everything. I was just so engrossed in their family dynamic, what drove them to each other and what kept them apart for all these years. It was a real treat to get to write about Celine, a strong-willed Latina who had to be a single mom for the first five years of her daughter's life while also working full-time—a lot of her struggles were inspired by what I've seen in my life and from my mother.

And if you like this one, consider diving into *The Vet's Convenient Bride*, where Maria gets to find her HEA!

Luana <3

THE SECRET SHE KEPT FROM DR. DELGADO

LUANA DaROSA

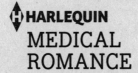

HARLEQUIN

MEDICAL
ROMANCE

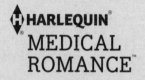

HARLEQUIN®
MEDICAL
ROMANCE™

Recycling programs
for this product may
not exist in your area.

ISBN-13: 978-1-335-59495-2

The Secret She Kept from Dr. Delgado

Copyright © 2023 by Luana DaRosa

Harlequin Enterprises ULC
22 Adelaide St. West, 41st Floor
Toronto, Ontario M5H 4E3, Canada
www.Harlequin.com

Printed in U.S.A.

Once at home in sunny Brazil, **Luana DaRosa** has since lived on three different continents, though her favorite romantic location remains the tropical places of Latin America. When she's not typing away at her latest romance novel or reading about love, Luana is either crocheting, buying yarn she doesn't need or chasing her bunnies around her house. She lives with her partner in a cozy town in the south of England. Find her on Twitter under the handle @ludarosabooks.

Books by Luana DaRosa

Harlequin Medical Romance

Amazon River Vets

The Vet's Convenient Bride

Falling for Her Off-Limits Boss
Her Secret Rio Baby
Falling Again for the Brazilian Doc

Visit the Author Profile page at Harlequin.com.

For my mum, who had to go through motherhood
mostly on her own and yet never gave up.

CHAPTER ONE

'WHAT DO YOU MEAN, he said *no*?'

Even though fury thundered through her at the news she had just received, Celine immediately regretted raising her voice. When it came to Darius, her fuse these days was rather short.

'I don't know what else to tell you.'

The voice on the other end of the phone belonged to Sebastião, a lawyer Celine had hired on the recommendation of Rafael, her brother-in-law.

'We tracked him down, sent the papers to him in Peru and now his lawyer just got in touch with me, saying that his client won't sign the papers like that.'

'I haven't seen this man in six years. How can he *refuse* to sign the divorce papers?' Nearly six years ago, Celine had made a grave mistake—she'd trusted her boyfriend enough to let him talk her into marriage. His mother, who held the visa for herself and Darius, had decided that it was time for them to leave Brazil. Darius had been in the final year of med school while Celine had just finished veterinary school. They had been seeing each other for two years, and the conversation around marriage had come up before. So when he'd asked her to get married so he could stay with her, she hadn't hesitated to say yes.

And then he'd left for Peru to sort out his return to Brazil with a new visa—and let her know only two days after his departure that he wouldn't be coming back and that she shouldn't contact him any more.

'I'm trying to dig into this issue with a Peruvian colleague. Clearly, our threatening letter didn't inspire any action.' Sebastião went quiet for a moment before he spoke again. 'Why wouldn't he want to sign the papers? Because of Nina?'

'Nina? No, he doesn't know he has a daughter. And now I'm not sure I want to tell him about her either.' When his message arrived that he wasn't coming back, she had tried everything to contact him despite his request not to do so. Celine had called, texted, written letters and tried to get friends to deliver messages for her—had redoubled that effort when she'd realised she was pregnant. But the other side of the line stayed quiet.

'What do we do next?' Impatience strained her voice. She had finally summoned the courage to ask for a divorce, burying the last remnants of her love for him, and now he *refused* to let her go? When he wasn't even in the country?

'You can still sue for divorce. It will just take longer. The court will assign you a date to speak in front of a judge, and that's when Darius will need to defend his refusal.' Sebastião paused as Celine sighed, frustration bubbling in her chest.

'All right, thank you, Sebastião. I appreciate your help. Please let me know what I can do to get done as fast as possible.'

'I'll be back in touch soon. Hang in there. We'll get this sorted.'

Celine hung up the phone, collapsing onto the chair in the kitchen. She'd been pacing up and down when Sebastião had called her. Exhaustion clamped its iron fist around her chest, making her feel wearier than she had in the last couple of weeks.

What had driven her to seek a divorce after six years of silence? She'd given up hope ages ago, focusing on her daughter and building a life for her—a life she was proud of, despite the struggles of a single mother.

The answer to her question strolled in through

the front door. Her sister, Maria, looked at her with raised eyebrows. 'Who ruined your day?'

Celine put her phone on the table and leaned forward, burying her face in her hands as she let out a long groan. 'Take a guess.'

'What happened?' Maria sat down in the chair next to her.

You happened, Celine thought, but didn't let those words pass her lips. It wasn't Maria's fault that she had found someone to share her life with. For the longest time the Dias sisters had shared this house, working alongside each other in their animal rescue and shouldering care for their children together.

Celine had been overjoyed when Maria found Rafael to fill a gap in her life she'd seen more clearly when things were quiet around them. It was their partnership that shone a glaring light on the problem she hadn't been dealing with in the last six years.

'Apparently Darius doesn't want to get divorced,' she said as she dropped her hands from her face.

Maria sucked her breath in. 'You spoke to him?'

'No. His lawyer spoke to my lawyer. Now we have to go to court to get this whole thing sorted out.' She sighed again, her eyes dropping to her hands splayed out on the table.

Maria frowned, leaning closer to pat her sister on the arm. 'We'll get through this. So the selfish jerk added another few months to the dissolution of your marriage. We've come so far, we can do this.'

Something inside Celine bristled at her sister's words. Though she had thought worse things of him, hearing someone else call him selfish set a deep-seated defence instinct loose in her. Even years later, the fragments of the relationship they had shared roared to life at the most unexpected times.

It wasn't as if her sister was wrong. What else could you call a man who ran away from the woman he had just married?

'Maybe this is just not worth the effort. I don't plan on getting married ever again, and I don't have time to think about men. Thanks to you, our charity has a shot at the future again.' Though she meant to sound cheerful, Celine couldn't keep the bitter edge from her voice. Before her sister had met Rafael, the two of them had run their animal charity together. Though that dream had always been more Maria's than Celine's. No, she had come here because of the heartache Darius's sudden desertion had caused her.

With Rafael to support Maria now, Celine had to admit that her role had significantly diminished, and she was more of a consultant than anything else.

'Don't give up, Cee. He doesn't get to hold you to this marriage when he isn't even a part of your life.' Maria crossed her arms in front of her chest and huffed out an annoyed breath. 'Men are twisted.'

'Oh, look who's talking—with your perfect husband and cute baby.' Celine mustered a laugh when a faint blush streaked over her sister's high cheekbones.

The door opened again and, as if summoned, Rafael stepped in, looking at them with a smile on his face. He was carrying a car seat in his hand, and the second Celine saw the sleeping face of her niece all the anger and frustration sitting in her chest melted away. Rafael set their daughter down and laid a hand on Maria's shoulder, giving it a gentle squeeze as he brushed a kiss on the top of her head.

This was why she wanted a divorce. She wanted a shot at *this*.

'Speak of the devil,' Celine said, but returned the smile her brother-in-law gave her.

'Ah, if you are at the part of your evening where you gossip about me, I think that's a good time to call it a day—or I will never get her out of here.'

Maria laughed and got up from her seat.

They both bade her goodnight, and as Maria grabbed the baby carrier from the floor Rafael turned around to look at her.

'Oh, I almost forgot. Someone came by this morning to see you, but you weren't in.'

Celine furrowed her brow, thinking. She hadn't received any kind of message from her patients. While Rafael and Maria worked mainly in their vet clinic, Celine spent a lot of time travelling from place to place, tending to larger livestock in the area. This meant unpredictable work hours and that she might not be around for regular visits to their clinic. But who would even seek her out like that?

'Did they say what they wanted? I haven't received any calls.'

Rafael shook his head. 'No, he just asked to speak to you but wouldn't say anything else. I told him to try his luck in the evening.'

'Did he leave a name?' Who would have reason to visit her unannounced?

Rafael looked away for a second. 'Sorry, I didn't ask for the name. We were busy with an emergency when he came in. I just told him to come back in the evening.'

'I see, thanks for letting me know.' Celine saw them out and closed the door behind them, thinking about the mysterious visitor Rafael had mentioned. Her patients' owners never came to visit her here.

Was it someone unrelated to her work? That wasn't much more likely either. She travelled so much for work, Celine didn't really have friends in town that would just drop by to see her.

A knock on the door pulled her out of her contemplations, and her gaze darted around for a second. Had they left something behind?

'I don't see anything lying around,' she shouted as she moved to open the door. 'What do you—'

Her brain stopped working mid-sentence as she stared into a face from the past that had been haunting her for the last six years.

'Darius…'

A whirl of different emotions tore through Darius as he sat watching the house where his estranged wife lived. When he'd come here to talk to her, he hadn't imagined being stuck in his car, watching her from afar as he contemplated what to tell her.

Can we please not get divorced for another three months because I need the visa for my job?

That wasn't going to win him her favour—and he really needed her to help him. Not that he had any favours left with Celine. But he needed to ask her anyway, even though he suspected she would send him packing and all his plans for a future in Brazil would collapse with that.

Not that he didn't deserve it. The pain of leaving Celine all those years ago had left a hole in his chest that had never closed in the years he'd spent away.

He'd left Brazil intending to come back as soon as he had sorted his spouse visa out, but when he'd told his mother about it she had revealed the real reason they had left. She had initially claimed that it was because of an advantageous business deal back in Peru. After his father's sudden death over twenty years ago, his mother had founded Delgado Cosmetics to keep her and her son fed. Though she'd initially worked out of their small kitchen, the brand had gained acclaim for its high standard in skincare and had become popular in Brazil—which had been the reason for their move there.

But apparently after years of success, the sales had waned, leading to his mother making riskier investments and borrowing money from people she shouldn't have. The result had been her fleeing the country from her creditors, and telling Darius that he too was in great danger if he returned to Brazil as the people she had got involved with would not shy away from hurting him—or his new wife, were they to ever learn about that connection.

Fearing what the loan sharks would do to Celine, he had kept quiet, even though it had torn him up inside.

Darius sat up when the door opened and two shadowy figures walked out, waving at the woman standing against the light of her house. Celine.

He gritted his teeth when a flood of ancient emotions broke through parts of the dam he'd erected inside of him to stem any feelings that lingered for this woman. He'd spent a lot of time shutting them away, never to think about them again—but now the culmination of his dreams depended on their marriage. Would she agree to stay married to him just for a while? Would she even hear him out?

The chances were slim, but Darius had to try.

He watched the two people get into their car and drive off. Taking deep breaths, he forced himself into motion, getting out of his car and crossing the short distance between the street to the small building nestled against the back of the main house—the vet clinic her parents had run before they'd retired.

He'd been surprised to learn that she had returned to Santarém to be a part of the charity her family had been running for decades. Her sister, Maria, had been the one with the dream to take it over, but when Darius and Celine had spoken about their future together, Santarém had never once come up. His estranged wife had even said that she wanted to distance herself from the charity to give her older sister the time in the spotlight she deserved.

Had she come back because of him? Because his absence had rendered their future plans obsolete?

Nervous energy trickled through him when he stood in front of the door, staring at a worn wooden plaque with her family name engraved on it. Dias.

He swallowed the lump building in his chest as he raised his hand and knocked on the door. Behind it, he heard her muffled voice calling out, and then the door flew open again. 'What do you—'

The words stopped as she stared at him—in confusion at first. Clearly, he wasn't the person she'd expected on the other side. No one really expected their long-estranged husband to suddenly show up one evening.

The moment understanding dawned on her face and he saw the pain flicker alive in her eyes he felt his breath leave his body as he sensed her agony in his own bones.

'Darius…' She said his name with a mixture of emotions too complex to unravel. Hurt—so much of it—wrapped itself around each syllable. But as her voice cracked, a sense of long-forgotten longing seeped through as well, matching the ancient memories resurrected in his own chest.

'Hey, Cee.' He didn't know what else to say. He'd flown here from São Paulo, where he worked as the head physician for one of the premier football clubs of the Brazilian league, and had agonised over what he would say when they finally met face to face.

But nothing had prepared him for the visceral reaction that erupted through him as he saw her stand in front of him. Six years had taken the budding beauty he'd seen in her and honed her into a woman so stunning he couldn't understand what she'd ever seen in him.

For a second her features remained soft, reminiscent of the love they'd once shared, and all the memories of their relationship came rushing back into the space between them. Darius felt a tug on his hand, calling it upwards to touch her cheek. But the moment was fleeting. Not even a heartbeat later, her expression changed into one hewn out of stone.

'You'd better be here to sign those divorce papers,' she said, her voice coated in ice so tangible his skin prickled.

'Yes, that's why I'm here. I just wanted to talk to you first.' This was the truth he was willing to go with. She hadn't asked if he wanted to sign the divorce papers *right now*. And he was going to sign them as soon as the current football season was over and he could convince the team's owners to sponsor his visa.

A subject he needed to broach with her today.

'*Now* you want to talk? After six years of silence and missed phone calls, you want to have a normal conversation like nothing ever happened?'

Darius bit his lip to stop the sigh building in his chest from escaping. He knew when he'd first arrived that this conversation wouldn't be an easy one, especially remembering one trait they had in common, which had also fuelled the fire of their relationship—they could both be incredibly stubborn over the most minute things.

'We're already not having a normal conversation, and I don't know when I gave the impression that I thought any of this was ordinary,' he replied through gritted teeth. 'If you give me some of your time, maybe I can start grovelling so you can finally find some closure. I'm not here because I want you back.'

He didn't know if it was necessary to state this, but he wanted to ensure that this question was out of the way. While his heart was pounding against his chest from being so near to the woman he'd desired so fiercely, he knew he couldn't have her—didn't want to either. Though he'd believed he had good reasons to stay away from her—his mother's lies around her financial problems only exposed with her death—he'd been a coward for leaving and he couldn't forgive himself for that.

And, by the look on her face, she wasn't close to forgiving him either.

'I certainly hope so. I'd have to call someone if you told me this is some strange romantic gesture.'

'Maybe if I can have some of your time…' Darius left the rest of the sentence unsaid, daring to meet her gaze. He couldn't help but marvel at the amber of her eyes that was only interrupted by smatterings of dark dots, almost as if they were trying to form a constellation in her iris. Darius had spent countless hours looking into those eyes, counting the little flecks.

'I can't talk here,' she finally said, her gaze

darting over her shoulder for a second. 'How long are you going to be here?'

Darius paused, hope blossoming in his chest. This wasn't a hard no. He might be able to convince her—to apologise for lacking the courage a real husband needed.

'I'm on leave for the next week. The team is finishing up the Copa América, so they are training with the national team.'

'The Copa? What are you—' Steps shuffling on the far side of the house interrupted her. Celine looked back again before taking a step forward and pulling the door closed behind her. 'I'm driving to a farm tomorrow to examine some livestock. You can come with me, and we can talk in the car.'

'Are you with someone?' The question flew from his mouth before he could contemplate how it was really none of his business, yet the edge in his voice shook him on a deeper level. While they were technically married, Celine had, of course, moved on with her life.

Was that why she had sent him the divorce papers? Because she wanted to get married to someone else? The thought caused a dissonance within him he didn't want to inspect closer. Darius had been the one to leave— regardless of the good reasons he'd had, he'd left her to pick up the pieces on her own.

'What if I am? My *husband* hasn't really been in the picture for the last six years.' She gave voice to the inner monologue in his brain when he'd asked the question.

He shook his head, not wanting to delve into this topic. The fury boiling in his veins stemmed from ancient affection that needed to remain long-forgotten for them to have a somewhat civil discussion. Darius wasn't here because of love. Though he'd never been able to bury his feelings for Celine, he was here to save his dream and give her—and himself— some closure.

He owed her the truth, no matter how painful it was.

'I'll come with you,' he said with a nod, not wanting to let the olive branch she extended go. This might be the only chance he had to tell her why he'd left and how he needed more time before he signed the papers.

'I'm leaving early tomorrow. Be here at six and we can talk. Stay in your car until you see me walk towards mine, then meet me there. I don't want anyone to see you loitering around my house.' Her voice was still frosty, but beneath the hurt he could glimpse the Celine who had agreed to marry him so they could be together—even though he'd learned that things weren't as simple as that.

She was still so much like the person he'd fallen in love with. It was hard to keep the old affection at bay. Darius reminded himself that he'd come here for a purpose, and it wasn't to fall in love again. No, he needed time to figure his life out, and he prayed that she'd grant him that time.

Three months until the season ended. That was all he needed.

CHAPTER TWO

CELINE TOOK A sip of her coffee, hoping that it would stave off the dread pooling in the pit of her stomach. Last night's surprise visitor had shaken her to her core, leaving her with a deep sense of inner turmoil that had kept her awake for a considerable portion of the night.

Darius was back—and he wanted to talk.

It was something Celine had wanted for many years, longing to get some sense of closure after what had happened. Because he'd been staying in Brazil under his mother's visa, he'd had to leave with her even after they'd got married so he could reapply for a spouse visa. Though it had been hard to say goodbye, she'd known it would only be for a few weeks before he'd return and no one could take him from her again.

The last thing she had expected was for Darius to be the one to end their relationship. His message had been vague, telling her he no longer wished to come back, but didn't explain why. Didn't give her an opportunity to fight for him either.

And another four weeks later Celine had received news that changed her life—and made Darius's departure that much more painful.

The thought of Nina brought the nervous energy to a boil. Darius didn't know he had a five-year-old daughter. That was something she would have to bring up with him. His reaction would tell her everything she needed to know about who he'd become in the last six years.

Though Celine had always remained light on the details, she'd told Nina that her father was away, and that he wouldn't be around. She would need to tell her about him too. How would she even go about having such a conversation? Before she could mention Darius's reappearance to their daughter, she needed to understand why he'd chosen to come back into her life rather than just signing the papers.

'Good morning, Mãe.' Celine looked up from her coffee as her daughter walked into the kitchen. Still wearing her pyjamas, she rubbed one hand over her eyes, lids still heavy with sleep.

'You're up early, *amor*.'

Nina only shrugged, then climbed onto the

chair next to hers before putting her hands on the table and resting her head on top of them.

'Are you hungry?' Celine asked, then got up when her daughter nodded.

She grabbed a bowl from the cupboard and poured cereal into it. 'I'm off to vaccinate some livestock. They have a lot of animals to get through, so I'm starting early. Tia Maria will be over in a moment to watch you before taking you to kindergarten.'

She put the bowl of cereal in front of her daughter and grabbed the soy milk from their fridge, giving the carton a swift shake before pouring it out. Nina grabbed the spoon and dug in, filling the kitchen with the sound of quiet chewing.

With her daughter somewhat distracted, Celine stepped to the window and peered outside to see a car pull over, and Maria step out of it. But there was another car parked further down that she didn't recognise. Its windows were tinted, so she couldn't see who was sitting in it either. Was that Darius?

She turned away when her sister opened the door, letting herself in with her own key. 'Good morning, sweetie,' she said before her eyes found Celine.

Her eyebrows shot up. 'You okay?' she asked,

clearly seeing something in her face that Celine didn't want her to see.

'Yeah, all good. Just a long day ahead of me and not looking forward to it,' she said as an excuse and, before Maria could ask anything else, she rushed over to the door, shouldered her bag and grabbed her keys. 'I'm off, my sweet. Your aunt will take you and your cousin to school today, so don't dally with your breakfast.' She hurried over to kiss Nina on the top of her head then left, slamming the door just a bit too hard.

She felt bad keeping Darius's presence from her sister, but she needed time to process it herself. Over the last few years Maria had been invaluable, keeping her sane throughout her unexpected pregnancy and taking care of Nina whenever she needed her to. Celine tried to give back to her sister as much as possible, spending time in the clinic whenever she could—less since Rafael had arrived.

That was a debt she didn't know how to repay.

When she reached her truck she threw the bag in the back seat and looked over her shoulder towards the house. The window in the kitchen was lit, but she didn't see Maria standing at it, watching her. Good. She didn't want to have the Darius conversation yet. Not when she herself was trying to figure it out.

Her eyes flitted to the unknown car and, as if he'd been waiting for some sort of signal, Darius emerged from it and strode towards her, the car lights flashing as he locked it with a remote. Celine's stomach gave a pitiful rumble as he came closer, his gait enough to elicit memories of a marriage that had lasted only a few days. If only the years had been unkind to him, she thought as she raised her chin. But whatever life he had lived in Peru had clearly done him well.

While the old sneakers and the worn-out jeans were appropriate attire for their morning outing, the expensive watch and light brown hair styled to perfection gave away the success he'd found as a person. Hair that was short on the sides and longer on top, begging to be ruffled through with longing fingers.

'Buenos dias,' he said when he got into the passenger seat of her car. And along with the perfect picture of masculinity and poise came the subtle scent of pine and spices, transporting her thoughts to the last place she'd smelled that combination—wrapped up in Darius's arms on the night of their courthouse wedding as they'd made love for the first time as a married couple.

Bad. This was very, *very* bad. He was the one who'd run away from his responsibilities after asking her to marry him. She should not be indulging any old memories of a time when their love was real—when she'd thought nothing could defeat them because she would have never believed Darius to be the one to break them apart.

'Darius.' She gave a curt nod and bit her lip as her traitorous body reacted to his proximity as if he had some kind of magnet that overpowered her free will with a mere glance.

'That's what you drive around in the countryside?' she said as she eyed his expensive car, imagining it covered in mud after a few hours driving around rural Brazil.

'It's a rental car. What do you expect? At least it's better than the club car I drive in São Paulo,' he replied.

'Club car?' Celine shook off the tension gripping her chest, focusing on what he had just shared. Though the urge had been strong, she had used every ounce of stubbornness within her to resist stalking her estranged husband on the internet, knowing heartache was all it would bring her.

A stranger might as well have stood in front of her, that was how little she now knew the man she had married. A tingling sensation flowed from her hands down her arms and into her belly, pooling there in a coil of warmth and nervous energy.

This was so not happening to her. This was the man who had left her pregnant and alone mere days after marrying her, not once answering any of the hundreds of her calls or texts. There was no way the thing stirring right behind her belly-button was genuine attraction. It had to be some old memory that was now rearing its head at the sheer familiarity his presence brought back into her life.

'I'm the head physician for a *futebol* team in São Paulo,' he said, bringing her back to her question.

She stuck the key into the ignition but stopped mid-turn to look at him. 'You finished med school in Peru?'

A line appeared between his brows. 'Yes, of course. Why do you sound horrified at that?'

'Because...' Her voice trailed off as she searched for the right words. 'You left. You ran from your responsibilities, from your wife, and then what? You just moved on with your life and finished med school?'

The words came forth without a filter and Celine didn't dare to look at him, afraid of what she might see in his face. She started the truck instead and began the journey to the farm. At least driving gave her a good excuse to keep her eyes off him.

'Cee, I—how do you expect me to respond to that? I'm sorry for what I did, and I'm not asking for your forgiveness. The way I hurt you—it's unforgivable. But I mean to look you in the eye when I apologise. You need to see that I mean it, that it's not just empty words.' From the corner of her eye she saw his chest rise and fall with a great heave, speaking of the effort this apology had taken from him.

Good. It wouldn't be a genuine apology if he wasn't struggling with it.

'Why?' It was the one question burning on her tongue, one word with so many answers outstanding.

Darius heaved a great sigh, his head dipping down as he rubbed his hands over his eyes. The weariness in his features was new. During their student romance he'd been the daring one, always looking for their next adventure, while Celine tempered his wilder ideas.

Something had happened to him that had forced him to leave. The naïve, hopeful part of her heart that still remained intact had clung to that narrative in her darkest hour, shielding her from the potential truth that he had never really loved her.

But what would have been so bad that he couldn't tell her?

They drove past lush green fields, a few of them fenced, with grazing cows and alpacas that had ventured far enough for one to see from the side of the road. Most of the landscape here was dedicated to grain farming to keep the population of livestock fed. The surroundings weren't quite the same as the dense trees of the rainforest that wound itself through the land alongside the Amazon River. But, unlike her sister, who was at home in the forest and dedicated their animal charity to the animals who lived there, Celine preferred the structure and schedule of the farm over the chaos of the wild.

The familiar view was a comfort to her as the silence in the truck grew longer.

Finally, Darius took a deep breath and said, 'My mother...she was sick, though I only learned that once I told her I was planning to go back to Brazil and be with you. She'd forced us to leave the country under...other circumstances, but in the end she wanted to be back in Peru for her health.'

The sign pointing at the road to the farm popped up on the side, a wooden plaque that welcomed everyone who drove by in big cursive letters. This was usually when the excitement to see everyone on the farm grew the closer Celine got. But it was as if her mind hadn't registered the sign, focused too much on her estranged husband sitting next to her and finally revealing the truth.

Darius too noticed the sign, glad that they would soon arrive. His eyes kept darting to Celine, but with her gaze trained on the road it was hard for him to gauge her reaction.

The truth—the entire truth—clung to his lips, but when he willed himself to say the words they wouldn't come to him. His mother had been sick, that *was* the reason she had wanted him to stay in Peru with her. But what had kept him there had been the web of lies she'd spun around him. The potential threat to Celine had been too great a risk for him to take.

Darius knew she deserved to know the truth, yet still he hesitated. Would she even believe him? The optics weren't in his favour, and if he put himself in her position he wasn't sure if *he* would believe his story either. After all, outwardly, his mother had been a successful businesswoman.

Would Celine judge him for believing his mother? Though he had acted on what he'd thought was true information, he couldn't deny the hurt he had caused. How could he ask for forgiveness when he himself struggled with what he had done? The guilt of his abandonment sat deep in his heart, but he didn't dare to let her see it.

No, the truth would only soothe his own guilt. It wouldn't give her anything. Better to let go of her, of the idea of their marriage, and carry the truth in his heart. He had nothing to gain from disturbing her again, of telling his side of the story. What if she did forgive him? Darius couldn't let her waste her time with him, not when his judgement and decision-making had been so wrong in the past.

What if he'd got other things wrong?

Celine didn't reply to his response, instead driving in silence until the tiled roofs of buildings appeared on the horizon as they approached the top of the hill where the farm was located. Several white-walled houses dotted the landscape, each one a different size to fit its purpose. They kept heading up the dirt road until they came to a halt in front of what could only be the main house.

Celine pulled the handbrake up, taking the key out of the ignition, but remained in her seat. Finally, she turned her head to look at him, her expression veiled. 'Your mother was sick?'

'She was, yes,' he said, and his heart rate took a tumble when he looked at her.

'And…' She hesitated, a hint of something intangible weaving itself through that word. Her throat bobbed as she swallowed before she continued. 'And you thought you couldn't tell me that?'

'What? No, I—'

'Then *why* did you not tell me? Why did you let me believe it was my fault? Why did you not pick up the phone?'

The last words weren't much louder than the others, but the pain in them amplified their sound as if a thunderstorm had struck right next to him. Her hurt cut him to the bone, leaving him stunned and staring at her with wide eyes.

'Celine, I thought we could—'

She cut him off again when she realised he wasn't giving an actual answer. 'There was a time when you'd tell me anything, but when it actually counted you couldn't open your mouth. Did you think I wouldn't understand? You thought so little of the woman you married?'

Her eyes swam with unshed tears, squeezing his chest so tight that all the air fled his lungs. His lips parted, but no words formed in his mind. Everything he had in him focused on the torment etched in her face. Darius had known this conversation would be painful. His chest tightened, the truth wanting to spill out into the open. But he couldn't let it out—not when it was only going to serve him. He'd do it if it were for her, but she would only see it as another excuse, another reason why she should never have married him.

'Cee…'

'Why, Darius? You had six years to think about this. By now you should have an answer to—'

He was the one to interrupt this time. 'You don't know *everything* that happened, Celine! I had good reasons to keep things from you.' He swallowed the lump in his throat, his mouth dry from the effort it took him to keep his voice from cracking. 'The truth won't change anything between us because you already decided how you want to see me. Anything I have to say in my defence is futile, is it not? So let's just both agree that I messed up this marriage, and then we can start finding our way towards a divorce.'

Celine blinked twice, the mist in her gaze dissolving. Movement in front of them drew their attention away from this intense moment that had been in the making for years. A short woman opened the front door, waving with a big smile on her face.

Celine returned the wave with a plastered-on smile before looking back at Darius, the disquiet in her eyes setting off alarm bells in his head. 'I hoped you'd have enough respect for me to at least tell me the truth. But you're right. All I want is you out of my life.'

He opened his mouth, but Celine shook her head. 'Juliana is waiting for us.'

Darius gave a curt nod, then looked around and jumped out of the car, opening the hatch to take the heavy-looking bag.

'What are you doing?'

He glanced at the contents of the bag through the half-open zip. 'This looks like vaccinations. I'm a doctor. I know how to administer vaccinations.'

Celine snorted at that, and the sound hit him in a different, softer part of his chest. For a moment she looked almost exactly like he remembered her, even-tempered until someone or something slipped past her defences—to find an adorable goofball.

'You're a *human* doctor. We're vaccinating cows today.' Scepticism laced her voice and raised Darius's competitive spirit.

'So a slightly bigger mammal. I think if you show me how and where to poke the needle,

I'll be more help than hindrance.' He crossed his arms, nudging his chin forward in a challenge he knew she couldn't refuse. Six years might have passed—and maybe too much bad blood to repair their relationship—but he still knew this woman.

Her eyes narrowed, a dangerous sparkle entering those endlessly deep amber eyes. Then she turned around to face the woman approaching them.

'Juliana, good to see you,' she greeted her, stepping forward to give the woman a quick hug. 'This is Darius, my assistant.'

Juliana turned to Darius and held her hand out. The quick but firm handshake was enough to feel the calluses along her palms, a subtle but powerful sign of how much work she put into her farm. And from the grin spreading over her face, a similar understanding passed through her.

'I see you're a man who doesn't shy away from hard work,' she said with a nod, and Celine raised one of her eyebrows but didn't say anything.

'We're ready to get some cattle vaccinated. Are they in the barn?'

Juliana nodded, waving them along. 'Glad to see things are going better for you two now that you can afford some help. You won't have to spend all day here,' the farmer said, getting only a grunt back from Celine.

Better? Had she been in trouble? Darius furrowed his brow but said nothing, letting his gaze drift when he caught her glaring in his direction. Maybe if she thought him distracted she would let her guard down around Juliana.

He spotted the beginning of the fence denoting Juliana's property but, as his gaze followed it, it vanished behind the horizon, hinting at the vastness of the fields. Both alpacas and cows were grazing on green fields, the fragrance of fresh grass and dried hay enveloping them with every step. Brazil's humidity was much more oppressive out here, and it would only get worse with the rising sun.

'I want you to look at one of our horses as well. My daughter says there is an issue with Roach's foot. He's not lame, but she says she feels *something* when they ride,' Juliana said, and Celine nodded.

'Llamaste cucaracha a tu caballo?' Darius asked, his mouth faster than his brain.

The woman looked at him with raised eyebrows before looking back at Celine, who had a barely noticeable smirk on her face. 'Darius is from Peru, but he speaks Portuguese. He's surprised you would name your horse after an insect.'

'Ooh,' Juliana said, waving her hand dismissively. 'My daughter named the horse. It's from a video game or a TV show. I can't remember.'

Darius followed behind the women, shaking his head at the slip-up. He was more on edge than he had let himself believe if he lapsed into Spanish like that. Though he'd grown up speaking Portuguese, they'd always spoken Spanish at home, so much that people could still detect the hint of an accent if they listened closely.

They arrived at the largest of the several barns strewn around the property. The wide doors were already open and the sound of cows shuffling and mooing mixed with the smell of hay as they stepped in. Inside, the barn was divided into several pens in which the cows lived, each box large enough to accommodate several more than were currently inhabiting them.

A smile tugged on Celine's lips when he glanced over at her as she stepped closer to one pen and laid her hand on the wide forehead of a brown cow. Her fingers rubbed through the hair and the animal inclined its head to nuzzle closer at the affectionate touch.

Darius couldn't help but smile as well, the constant pulse of guilt fading away for a few moments as he observed the joy her work brought to her—wishing that he could have been there as she'd grown into her role as a veterinarian. The regret of missed opportunities came up his throat like bitter bile as another fragment of the life he'd lost came to life in front of his eyes.

Without the machinations of his mother, he might never have left and they would have had a chance at a genuine marriage. It was easy to blame his mother. He had only found out after her death that the loan sharks threatening her and her loved ones had been in her imagination—a ruse to keep him in check. But Darius needed to remind himself of the part he himself had played. After all, he'd chosen to leave—he'd been misled, but he'd left.

They stopped in front of a pen populated with calves. Some eyed them as they approached, but most remained with their heads down, nipping at the hay covering the ground.

'These are all?' Celine asked Juliana, who nodded.

'Yep, impressive, isn't it?' The woman sported a proud grin, eyeing both Darius and Celine as she waited for confirmation.

'You know how I feel about your gorgeous animals, Jules,' Celine said with a laugh.

She reached up to the door of the pen and undid the latch, pulling it open and waving

Darius along with her. 'I'll give them a quick exam followed by their vaccine. This shouldn't take too much time. Darius—' She pointed at the bag hanging from his shoulder.

'Come find me at the house once you're done,' Juliana said, leaving them with a wave.

Darius took the bag, placing it on a small table to the side that looked like it had been brought in for this specific occasion. When he went to open the zip Celine moved next to him and bumped him with her hip to move him out of the way.

Her scent enveloped him for a fraction of a second, drowning out the surrounding sounds and smells as awareness rushed through him. Old memories flashed through his mind, the same scent of spice and something primal cradling him to sleep as he'd held her against him.

But the look she gave him now as she glared over her shoulder was nothing like the ones she used to give him. The light and gentleness had been replaced by an impenetrable brick wall that he couldn't see beyond. Darius used to know exactly what she was thinking... Before his life had been upended by his mother's lies.

Before he had left.

They vaccinated the calves and Celine didn't find anything of note that warranted alerting

Juliana. All her new calves were happy and healthy. What she noted though was Darius through the entire process. His eyes had grown large when she had prepared the vaccination gun. Clearly he had expected cattle to be vaccinated just like humans, each one getting their own syringe.

But with a farm the size of Juliana's that endeavour would take several days if they had to go through all the resident animals. To be time-efficient, large animal vets instead used an apparatus that would fill a syringe with a predetermined amount of medication and a mechanism to change the needle after every shot.

Despite his claim in the car, Darius wasn't able to assist her with vaccinating the animals, though he did a tremendous job in calming the little calves as she worked her way through them. Watching him rub each calf behind its ears before they moved onto the next one while whispering encouragements to them ignited a warm and fuzzy feeling in the pit of her stomach that Celine was too scared to examine any closer.

Heat rose in her body as she watched him, a flame she hadn't felt flicker inside her since the day he'd left. The familiarity of it was almost enough to lure her back into his arms.

How could she be angry at a man who treated animals with such respect and empathy?

By remembering that he had left her and his child with only a message to let them know they would never see him again. Her chest squeezed tight when Nina came to her mind. She needed to tell him about his daughter, but fear surged through her veins when she thought about mentioning her. Their lives had been just fine without him. True, Santarém had never been the place she'd envisioned growing her family, but with the amount of help her sister had given her from the day she'd learned she was pregnant, she couldn't just up and leave because she felt like it.

Celine needed to know why he was here—and why he refused to sign the divorce papers.

'You handled the calves well for a people doctor,' she said, even though a myriad different words formed in her throat. But his bright eyes were so disarming she forgot about her apprehension for a few heartbeats.

'Is there something going on in the medical community that I'm unaware of? Are medical doctors and vets at war?' His tone was playful as he walked to the table with her bag on it, packing up the instruments she had used to examine the calves.

Celine didn't reply and watched him instead,

her eyes gliding down to those hands that had once held her so tight—made her feel so safe. How could all of that have been an illusion dreamt up by a love-addled young adult?

'You still haven't told me why you're here,' she said when they remained quiet.

Darius rustled around the bag, his eyes trained on his hands. The sound of the zip filled the air, only stressing the silence rather than masking it.

'Let me preface everything by acknowledging how much pain I caused you when I left. Nothing I can say will make it better, but I'm willing to put in the work to rebuild your trust.'

Celine furrowed her brow, her arms crossed. 'Trust? Darius, I will *never* trust you again, so don't waste both of our time. What I want is for you to sign these divorce papers and get the hell out of my life again.' She bit her lip when her voice trembled, cursing herself for showing such fury in front of him.

Memories of their relationship flashed through her mind whenever she let her thoughts wander. Things had been so much easier six years ago when they were in love. Ever the romantic, Celine's younger self knew she was meant to marry Darius and couldn't believe how lucky she was that she'd got to meet the love of her life at twenty-one without even trying.

'What if I told you I want to move back to Brazil for good?' he asked, and Celine stared at him as her pulse took a traitorous tumble at his words.

'What do you mean?'

He was coming back? A familiar heat rose through her body and to her cheeks at that information, leaving her at a loss for words. Why would she care if he was back? He had left her broken, unable to pick herself up. Unable to… move on, because how could she explain that she was stuck in a marriage that had lasted a few days total?

It was the reason Celine had waited so long to ask for a divorce. Her broken-down marriage had become a shield behind which she hid from any attention when her heart remained too broken to consider someone else by her side.

'That's the reason I came to see you. I'd been here a few weeks when my lawyer called to let me know that some papers had arrived—your divorce papers.' He zipped the front pockets of the bag closed and shouldered it again, looking at her expectantly when she didn't move. 'Should we go and see Cucaracha?'

'Oh…' Hearing the name of Juliana's horse snapped her back into reality and she nodded, walking out of the barn and to the stables a few metres further along.

'Why didn't you sign?' That was the question causing the lion's share of unease pooling inside of Celine. Why was he here instead of in his lawyer's office, signing the papers and finally letting her go?

'The club offered me the job under the condition that I start right away. It's a temporary contract, as their head physician had to leave somewhat abruptly. They said they wanted me, but they couldn't afford to wait for the visa process, not with the Copa ending so soon and their players coming back to the club.' He paused when they got to the stable and pushed the door open for them to enter.

'How does that concern me asking you to sign the divorce papers?'

She stopped in front of Roach's box, turning to look at the horse, her question to Darius forgotten. 'Hey, buddy. What's up with you today?' she greeted the animal, reaching over to her bag, still hanging from Darius's shoulder, to retrieve some treats.

She held her palm out flat, rubbing the ridge of Roach's nose as he snapped up the treats with a satisfied snort.

'There should be a black case in the bottom of the bag. Can you dig it out?' Celine unlatched the gate as Darius put the bag on the floor to find the requested item. She pulled the gate shut behind her, taking the case from him when he reached over to hand it to her.

Inside were all the tools she needed to inspect Roach's hooves. Darius leaned over the gate, watching as she tied the horse's halter to a hook on the wall and pulled one of his back legs off the floor, holding it between her thighs as she bent over it.

Celine put the open case on the floor, grabbing the clinch cutter and a compact hammer to straighten the nails with which a farrier had attached the horseshoe to the hoof. She grunted when the last nail came out and the shoe dropped onto the floor.

A tingling sensation crawled down her spine, and when she looked up she caught Darius staring at her with a soft expression, a slight smile pulling at his lips. The look on his face evoked more memories of a time long gone, when they were still in love.

'What?' she said, irritated at the heat rising to her cheeks. There should be no such reaction to him. Had her body already forgotten what damage he had wrought on her heart and soul?

'You're a farrier too?' he asked, and Celine wasn't sure if that was awe that she heard in his voice.

'It's sort of part of a large animal vet's training and sort of not. We speak a lot about different hooves, but the work of a farrier is an entirely different discipline. When I returned to Santarém the opportunity to work with the farmsteads in the area came up, which excited me more than the exotic animal work Maria does. So I took the time to apprentice with a farrier three years ago.'

She paused, putting the clinch cutter and hammer down, grabbing the hoof pick instead and started cleaning up the dirt and debris on the hoof in slow and precise downward strokes.

'I'm glad you get to do what you always wanted. You didn't seem to be enthusiastic about the rescue work, so I was worried you'd been forced into it when I realised you were back in your hometown,' Darius said from above her, renewing the heat that had just cascaded through her body.

He remembered that? Celine had never planned to come back to Santarém, not when she'd still thought that she and Darius would have a future together. But then he'd left, and shortly after she had learned of her pregnancy, and all her plans had been in pieces. At Maria's urging she'd come back to Santarém, so she could raise her child with the help of her sister. But she had never wanted to work at their family charity the way her sister had.

Why did Darius care at all about that? She didn't get to voice the question when she spotted something on Roach's hoof. With another grunt, she squeezed the hoof, some liquid coming to the surface from the area where the soft tissue of the hoof met the hard horn.

'Looks like we have a hoof abscess...' Celine mumbled, dropping the pick and grabbing the hoof knife instead to cut away at the excess sole as she narrowed down the location of the abscess.

It must be small, for Juliana hadn't mentioned anything about Roach avoiding standing on that leg. He didn't show any visible signs of discomfort, but that was difficult to tell with prey animals. Their natural inclination was to hide any pain, or they'd be left behind.

'Can you see if I brought any bandages? Antiseptic would be ideal, but I'll take any.' She didn't want to drain the abscess if they couldn't bandage Roach properly.

Darius's head disappeared as he ducked down to rummage through the bag, coming back up holding a large roll of bandages in a plastic bag.

Celine nodded with a smile. 'Okay, come in here. I'm going to cut a drain so the pus can flow out. We need to pack and bandage the hoof afterwards, so nothing gets into the wound.'

She dropped the hoof knife into the case, picking up a much smaller paring knife and squeezed the hoof again to see where to cut. Roach snorted above her, his tail swooshing back and forth as she worked on the hoof.

'Woah there, buddy. It's all good. You are doing so great. Just a bit longer and then you'll feel as good as new,' Darius mumbled above her, and Celine could feel the tension in the horse's body subsiding, making him more agreeable to her touch.

She swallowed the dryness spreading through her mouth, pushing away the unwanted sparks jumping around in her stomach. Now was not the time for her body to react to things her mind had already ruled out. The unbidden awareness of his presence was nothing more than a relic of their shared past—one she would soon be done with.

'All right, we're almost done here. Can you cut me a large length of the bandage?' she asked, passing him the scissors from her tool case.

'Well done, champion,' Darius said to Roach before he stepped back and cut the bandages to size, handing one to Celine each time she asked for it.

A few minutes later Roach's wound was dressed and they were on their way back to the main house.

'Thanks for your help back there. That would have been more difficult without you,' she said as she sent him a sideways glance.

The way he had soothed Roach when she was working on him had set off a different heat inside her, one that gently radiated inside her chest rather than the flashes of hot fire she'd tried her best to suppress all day. Though both were inappropriate and unwelcome.

'Glad I could help. I can see how treating animals is extra challenging. At least a human can tell you where it hurts. Here you had to rely on the intuition of Roach's rider to understand that something was off.' His fascination sounded genuine as he spoke, drawing her gaze back to him.

She slowed down her pace as she looked him over, seeing something akin to anguish in his eyes that drew her back to their discussion before she had checked on Roach's hoof. There was a reason he'd come here rather than let his lawyer do the talking.

'Why are you here, Darius?'

He stopped, forcing her to turn mid-step so she could keep looking at him.

'I came here as the spouse of a Brazilian citizen so I could start working straight away. I cannot get divorced because that would mean deportation.'

Celine blinked several times as his words sank in.

'You did *what*?'

'I need three months to show the team I'm the person they want for the job. Once the season is over, I can go back to Peru and apply for a work visa.' He sighed, his fingers grasping the strap of her bag so tightly she saw the whites of his knuckles appear. 'Please give me three more months, and then I will sign any paper you want.'

No. The word clung to her lips the moment Darius uttered that ridiculous request, fury and hurt blooming in her chest and drowning out the gentle warmth she had sensed there just moments ago. But, despite her vehement reaction, she couldn't say or do what she wanted in this very moment, acting on years of abandonment issues he'd caused in her. Because this wasn't just about her and how much she wanted Darius to leave her alone.

This was also about Nina, who had never met her father.

How would she be any better than her brother, Daniel, who had walked out on his daughter—Celine's niece Mirabel, who lived with Maria and her husband—if she didn't consider this opportunity for Nina? No matter how she felt about Darius, wouldn't it be good for her child to have her father in her life?

'Is your plan to stay in Brazil long-term?' she asked, wanting to know more about his plans before she committed to anything.

Telling Darius that he had a daughter would be an incredibly difficult conversation, one she'd been having in her head since he'd shown up at her door.

Celine had tried to inform him about being pregnant, but he had never picked up her calls, nor reacted to a single plea to phone her back. She could have texted him about it, but she hadn't wanted to. The news that they had created a life on their wedding night should come from her lips and not from a cheap text message.

But he hadn't picked up the phone, hadn't called her back, so she had never told him about their child.

Darius hesitated before he nodded. 'Yes. I want to work for this team.'

The conviction and passion entering his eyes as he spoke were almost enough to let her forget about the anger pumping through her veins, because it reminded her so much of the man she'd fallen in love with. If they hadn't been together, he'd been near a screen watching *futebol*. He'd expressed no interest in playing the game himself, happy enough being on the sidelines, and under any other circumstances Celine would have been glad that he'd found a career that let him do just that.

If he weren't the last person she wanted to see right now.

'Why did you choose to work for a Brazilian team?' she forced herself to ask. She was not entirely convinced of his good intentions, but for the sake of her—*their*—daughter, she had to try.

'Why I…' He stopped, head tilted, as he looked at her. 'Cee, I work for Atlético Morumbi.'

Her eyes rounded as the name unearthed a memory. Weeknights and weekends spent in their favourite bar in Manaus, surrounded by people wearing the black and white stripes of Morumbi. Discussions about how the new team manager had turned the team around and was bringing them to glory. Whispers in the dead of night of his dream to work with the team. She'd been excited for him back then, thrilled about the idea of living in São Paulo and building their careers there.

'Your father would be proud of you.' The words slipped past her lips unbidden and before she could give them more consideration. Though she had never met his father, as he had passed away long before they'd met, she knew from Darius that his father had played a role in his interest in Brazilian *futebol* even before the Delgado family had arrived from Peru.

'I…hope so,' Darius huffed, the rawness in his eyes so unexpected that her breath caught in her throat.

This side of him was too close, the vulnerability of the moment drawing her in. Because, deep down inside, she had never believed that her estranged husband was a bad person. But he had made a mistake she could not forget or forgive.

'You understand why I can't let this go, then? Why I had to come back here when I got the offer?' he asked, his voice a plea that sent a cold shiver down her spine.

She understood why he'd come back, and through the hurt his presence stirred in her Celine couldn't help but find a kernel of sympathy for him. There were a lot of things that she could be angry about regarding Darius, but following his dream wasn't one of them.

A sharp whistle tore through the air, and they both whipped around to see Juliana standing on her porch, waving at them. Celine shot a look at Darius and nodded to acknowledge what he had said, then started walking to where the farmer stood to give her a report on her animals.

'I'll come back tonight to drop off the pain medicine for Roach. The abscess was small and your kid caught it early. He should make a full recovery,' Celine said as she handed her the rest of the bandages.

'She's got that intuition from me,' Juliana said, pride puffing her chest. 'If yours and mine stay on the same trajectory, we'll be establishing a dynasty.'

A stone dropped into the pit of Celine's stomach. The perfectly innocent words turned her blood to ice, and she didn't dare look at Darius to see if he had understood what she had said.

'Sorry, Jules. We have to run to the next appointment, but I'll see you in the evening when I drop off the medicine.'

She didn't wait for the woman to reply, walking towards her truck and flinging herself into the driver's seat, the motor already running by the time Darius climbed into the passenger seat.

CHAPTER THREE

THEY'D DRIVEN BACK in silence, Celine still reeling from the request Darius had made of her. Three months. That was how long he wanted her to wait before he signed the divorce papers. Three months and then he would be out of her hair for ever. Except he wanted to stay in Brazil, and if he stayed here then maybe her daughter could finally have a father.

She had told him she needed to think about his request and invited him to come back the following day. The moment Celine stepped through the door she called Maria, who arrived twenty minutes later with a bottle of wine.

Pouring each of them a glass that contained a bit more wine than necessary, Celine plonked down on one of the kitchen chairs. Her geriatric Great Dane, Alexander, shuffled over to where the sisters were sitting, laying his large head on Maria's lap, and she scratched him behind the ear.

'You traitor,' Celine huffed as she took a big swig of her wine.

'Aww, did you miss me, Alexander?' her sister cooed, looking down at the dog with a familiar smile. Then she trained her eyes on Celine. 'So, what is the emergency?'

Celine took a deep breath, the wine already hot in the pit of her stomach as she searched for the courage to say the words she'd been carrying around in her chest the entire day.

The wine burned as she took another sip, setting the glass down with much more force than necessary. 'Darius showed up at my door last night,' she said, and Maria's eyes widened.

Stunned silence enveloped them for a few heartbeats, the soft breathing of their dog the only noise vibrating through the tiny kitchen. Then Maria's gaze flicked to the stairs at the far end of the room, past the living room.

'Where is Nina?' she asked, her voice tense.

'At a sleepover, thank God.'

'Did she see him?'

Celine shook her head. 'No. I stepped outside when he knocked on the door so she wouldn't overhear us.'

'Oh, wow…' Maria reached for her glass of wine for the first time since they'd started talking, rolling it around in one hand while the other still petted the dog's head on her lap. 'So…'

'Why did he come?' Celine finished her sentence.

'Yeah. I can't imagine he would show his face after all this time just to sign the divorce papers in person.'

Celine sighed into her glass, which was now almost empty. 'No, of course not. This man could not pick up the damn phone six years ago when I, *his wife*, needed to tell him about *our* daughter.'

'So what miracle brought this useless man into your life again?'

Even though Celine herself had called him much worse, her eyes shot up at her sister's description of Darius. Words of defence came to her lips, but she swallowed them with the last bit of wine remaining in her glass.

Darius had hurt her terribly, done the exact opposite of what he was supposed to do as her husband. Instead of struggling through everything—including his mother's sickness—together, he had shut her out and remained in Peru with no explanation. He *was* useless, yet Celine's immediate reaction had been one of defence.

He was *hers* to call as she pleased, no one else's. A tiny and yet intrusive thought that nestled itself inside her brain without permission. She should not feel possessive about Darius, the way she felt right now. It should not matter what Maria wanted to call him.

Yet it did.

'Apparently, he's been here for a while for work,' she said instead, willing her voice to remain neutral.

'Wait, here? In Santarém?'

Celine shook her head. 'He's working in São Paulo as the head physician for a football club.'

'He still became a doctor after he ran off?' The incredulous tone in Maria's voice hit another vulnerable spot inside Celine's chest that she didn't dare to examine too closely because she again wasn't wrong.

The way Darius had left didn't spark a lot of confidence in his reliability. Yet she knew this was what he'd dreamt of doing. Being the physician for Atlético Morumbi was the culmination of hard work and dedication, showing his tenacity and devotion to his dream. Even with all the hurt floating in the space between them, she couldn't deny him that credit. No, she only wished he had applied that same grit to their marriage.

'Okay, lay off him a bit, please.' The words shot out of her mouth before Celine could even contemplate their origin, yet alone decide if she wanted to say them.

Where was this sympathy coming from? After all the absent years with missed anniversaries, birthdays and major life events, she shouldn't even give him the time of day, yet alone defend him in front of Maria, who'd been the one to pick up the pieces when he'd left.

Her sister seemed to share the same thought, for a line appeared between her brows as she scrutinised her. 'Why?'

A question that expanded the size of the lump inside her throat. Because she didn't know why. The defensive feeling made no sense to her, yet it overpowered everything else and welled up strong enough that she had to say something about it. There was one reason—the only reason Celine was even talking about this whole charade as if she *might* agree to it.

'Because if Darius wants to stay in Brazil permanently, then that's a chance for Nina to finally have her father in her life. Six years late still seems better than not at all.' She had to try to put her complicated feelings for her estranged husband aside for the sake of her daughter—their daughter.

Maria frowned, closing her long and delicate fingers around her wineglass for the first time.

The white-gold wedding band on her left hand caught the dim light of the kitchen and sparkled, and Celine caught her breath. The sight crushed her deeply wounded heart as longing surged within her.

What Maria had found in Rafael... Celine had once believed herself and Darius to be just like that. Now she knew better, but that didn't stop the longing from rearing its demanding head whenever she saw her sister and brother-in-law around the vet clinic. She was so happy for them, and after how hard Maria had fought to keep their animal charity going she deserved every chance of happiness she set her heart on.

But it still stung seeing every day what she couldn't have. Not that she had looked very hard. Her job meant she travelled for several hours, sometimes days, to get to the remote farms scattered across central Brazil. But even though there had been opportunities to meet someone else, strangers she met on the road or people associated with the farms she serviced, there hadn't been anyone else—ever.

None of the people she met had ever inspired her to sort out the divorce until Maria had brought Rafael into their lives and reminded her of what life could be like with that one person by her side.

And now Darius—the man who was supposed to be that person to her—was back, and that longing that had been quietly brewing inside her chest had burst alive with an unexpected ferocity that left her almost paralysed with fear.

'How do you know Darius wants to be involved?' her sister asked.

'I don't know that he will. But I've decided to give him the three months that he needs… and I will give him the choice to get to know his daughter in that time. The alternative is to leave and never show his face in my life again.' She'd had it all planned out on the way back from Juliana's farm. She would give him three months, but he'd also get a choice. He could get to know his daughter, or he could leave and never come back.

'Have you told Nina already?'

Celine shook her head. 'No, I haven't told her yet. I want to talk to him first and only if he agrees will I bring it up with her. I don't want to get her hopes up, just for him to say no.'

'That won't be a comfortable conversation… He won't be happy about you keeping this to yourself for so long,' Maria mumbled into her glass as she took another sip.

That was something Celine had thought about as well, but she'd ultimately decided that she could weather his anger because he only had himself to blame. She'd *wanted* to tell him, had tried many times to reach him, until the strain and heartbreak of his abandonment had become too much and she'd given up trying. Darius had every opportunity to be in his daughter's life early on, and he'd made his decision by not answering her messages.

Maria shook her head and then laughed, the sound laced with the same incredulity Celine felt herself. 'Sounds like you've got your work cut out for you. I guess that means I have to make nice with Darius when he finally shows his face again.'

The displeasure in her sister's voice was apparent and, in this moment, she loved her for that. Because Maria understood what the idea of finally giving Nina access to her father meant to her.

'I've invited him here tomorrow to talk. We'll see how it goes after that.' Celine sighed, dropping her forehead into her hand and rubbing her temple with her thumb and index finger.

This would be painful for everyone involved.

Nervous energy pooled in the pit of his stomach when Darius arrived the next day around noon. Celine's message had given him no further sign of her decision.

Celine hadn't said no, which meant that his dream yet lived. Darius was so desperate to make this work, he was willing to promise her the stars and the moon if she only gave him three more months. Though the more likely wish she'd have for him was to never see his face again.

Something he was willing to give her as well, though the thought that this might be what she asked for turned the sensation circulating around his stomach into solid ice, sending chilled waves through his body with every beat of his heart.

Seeing her again and spending the better part of his day with her yesterday had shaken him to his very foundation, leaving him adrift as he searched for something to ground himself, to remind himself of his true purpose for being here. When they had first started seeing each other Celine had woven a spell around him he'd thought to be no more than the exaggerated memories of a teenage boy's first love.

Yesterday had shown him that the spell was still very much in place, drawing his eyes to places he couldn't touch—his mind to places it didn't belong.

Attraction had sparked back to life as easily as if they had spent days apart rather than years. That was how natural it had felt to Darius to share the same space with her again. If he spent any more time near her, he might actually start to believe that reconciliation could be in the cards for them.

Something he knew to be impossible. While his body might still react to Celine all these years later, he knew better than to let himself walk down that path. He couldn't possibly hope for redemption after all he had done. It didn't even matter if she ever forgave him. He himself could not forgive how little courage and trust he'd shown when faced with the lies of his mother.

Celine deserved to be set free to find a man worthy of her affection. All he needed from her was three months.

Darius glanced at himself in his rear-view mirror, frowning at the dark bags underneath his brown eyes. The marks looked almost blueish against his dark brown skin, the agony that had robbed him of most of his sleep plainly written on his face. With a huff he got out of his car, taking a deep breath to steel himself as he walked the short distance to her house and knocked on the door. He heard muffled footsteps from the other side, and even though he had mentally prepared himself to see her again his breath still caught in his throat when she stood in front of him.

Instant awareness overloaded his system, his thoughts becoming clouded by the pull of remembered desire that screamed at him to grab her by the shoulders and kiss her, just to get one more taste from the lips he'd starved himself of for so many years.

Something wet and cold touched his hand, breaking their transfixed gazes as Darius looked down. An enormous hound sat next to Celine, his height reaching way past her hips even while sitting down.

'Well, hello,' he greeted the dog, who stared at him with calm but watchful eyes.

'This is our family dog, Alexander,' Celine introduced him, scratching a spot between his ears.

Darius couldn't help but chuckle at the name. 'I always find it strange when people give their pets people's names.'

'People don't have the monopoly on names,' Celine said as she stepped aside, inviting him into her home.

Memories of two nights before flashed up in his mind, when she had stepped outside and closed the door behind her. Had it been her dog that made the sound that prompted her to close the door?

He looked around, searching for clues that someone else lived here with Celine. The rustic wooden table in the kitchen had four chairs around it, but there were no indications that lunch had been served, making it hard to judge how many people might have eaten here.

The living room unfolded on the other side of the open-plan space, with a cosy three-seater couch that had a plaid blanket draped over its back. Bookshelves lined the walls, but the only titles he could make out from where he was standing were thick veterinary textbooks.

Darius's gaze drifted further along and landed on a small shoe rack that was tucked away in the corner that held shoes of two wildly different sizes. The larger, more practical ones seemed to be Celine's, but the smaller ones...

'And for you it's Alexander the Great Dane.' His head whipped around to look back at Celine, who had crossed her arms and stared back at him with a stubborn glint in her eyes that he remembered well.

'Alexander...the Great Dane.' He repeated those words, his tone laced with amusement as he beheld the dog. 'Did you or Maria come up with this name?'

'Actually, it was—' She interrupted herself,

her eyes going wide, and Darius could almost sense the piece of information she was intentionally withholding from him. It stung a lot more than he'd thought it would, even though he knew he didn't deserve her confidence or her trust.

His eyes darted back to the shoe rack, wondering what those small shoes meant. These were clearly children's shoes. Something trickled down his spine, settling in his stomach in an uncomfortable sensation. Had Celine found the person she wanted to start a family with, and those were the shoes of her child?

The thought rose in him like bile, leaving a bitter taste in his mouth that he had no way to justify. He couldn't possibly be angry at her for moving on from their relationship. He had, after all. When he'd worked for a football team in Peru there had been many times when he'd taken women to his room after an away match, either to celebrate or to blow off steam—depending on the team's results.

True, he'd let no one get further than a few nights with him if they *really* got along well, but he'd always been upfront about the fact that he wasn't available. So why would it hurt to imagine Celine in the arms of someone else?

His gaze flickered over her fingers, which she had entangled in front of her. There wasn't

a ring on her finger, nothing indicating someone else in her life except for the shoes. Even
the rest of the living area and kitchen were
conspicuously empty of anything that could
point towards the life she led.

'Who named the dog?' he finally asked,
even though he had convinced himself a second earlier that he wasn't going to ask. It was
none of his business.

'Maybe we should sit. I want to discuss what
you asked me about yesterday.' Celine pointed
towards the chairs around the dining table and
pulled one out to seat herself.

Darius followed her, pressure building in his
chest as if someone were sitting on his ster-
num. Each step he took, it became harder to
breathe. She had deflected his question. So
there was definitely someone else in her life.
Which meant that she didn't want to wait another three months for him to achieve his
goals. And why would she? Clearly her life
had turned out just fine without him.

'I didn't know how much I was asking of
you when I presented you with my idea yesterday,' he said, trying to get ahead of the rejection.

But Celine shook her head, her fingers once
again intertwined in a strangely nervous man-
ner that gave him pause. Why was *she* ner-

vous? He was the one putting his life's dream in her hands.

'When you told me you'd come back to Brazil using our marriage, I wanted to outright reject you. Because I thought if you could come back here and not let me know, not pick up the phone again, that you hadn't changed at all. Indeed, if I had never sent those divorce papers you wouldn't even have come here, would you?'

She paused to look at him, her voice so brittle that a lump appeared in his throat. Because, from his expression alone, she knew the truth. When Darius had come back to Brazil he had wrestled with the idea of reaching out to her to explain himself. But fear had always paralysed him, stopping him from making a decision.

'I thought about reaching out, but the reasons for calling you after so long seemed so self-serving. I thought you'd have moved on a long time ago and the only reason I would break the silence would be to assuage my guilt.' The words left his lips more evenly than he felt, something he was grateful for.

Celine took a couple of deep breaths while spreading her fingers wide in front of her, before pressing her palms onto the wood of the dining table. 'At least you got some of it right. I had moved on and definitely didn't need to know you had used our farce of a marriage to get back into the country.'

Her barbed words hit their mark with expert precision, but he steeled himself not to show the hurt on his face. Celine still hadn't said no and she was going through an awful lot of trouble just to tell him she didn't want to help him. No, he was certain she was going to agree to his proposed plan. She just needed to name her conditions—something Darius wasn't concerned about. If it meant he could stay here and convince the team that he was worth keeping for the next couple of seasons, then he would pay any price. Nothing meant more to him than that.

Celine sighed, shaking her head as she understood what he was hoping. 'Okay, so you know I didn't ask you here to say no. I'm willing to help. But you just need to know something before we continue.'

Darius nodded. He'd known she would have a counter-offer when he'd proposed his idea yesterday. Celine had always been the one to plan things, needing to know all the details and how things were going to be before she agreed to anything. In fact it had surprised him she'd even agreed to marry him, knowing nothing more than that he needed her if he wanted to stay in Brazil—something that was true again six years later.

'I…' Her voice trailed off, her tone becoming thick with an emotion he couldn't quite decipher. She cleared her throat and when she met his gaze again he took in a sharp breath at the depth of conflict swirling in her amber eyes.

'Cee, what is it?' His hand was halfway across the table in an instinct to comfort her—an instinct he'd believed long dead. Could this still be about his request? What would put her in such a state of nervous anguish?

'I have a daughter. Her name is Nina, and she was the one who picked the dog at the shelter. Maria and I share custody because Mirabel and Nina keep fighting over who he belongs to.' Her laugh was noticeably tense.

Darius's hand froze in the air and a moment later he retracted it, placing it back in front of him. So Celine had a child. But why was she telling him?

Something deep inside him stirred, a strange premonition that made his blood run cold as he put together the splintered pieces of the conversation, along with her inexplicable nervousness when she was the one holding all the cards in this deal.

There was no way that the idea rising in him,

squeezing all the air out of his lungs, could be true. It just couldn't be, because there was *no way* Celine would have kept this a secret from him for six years.

But why else would she bring up her daughter in this discussion, unless…

'Celine…' he said, his voice as thick as hers had been just a few moments ago. 'What are you trying to tell me?'

His breath trembled when she looked at him, hurt mixing with remorse as she sucked her lower lip between her teeth, her chin shaking with her own unsteady breathing.

'Four weeks after you told me you wouldn't come back I realised I was pregnant, and I had her and raised her on my own.'

CHAPTER FOUR

THE SILENCE BETWEEN them was deafening, and Celine didn't dare to breathe as she waited for his reaction. She'd known it would be bad from the moment she'd realised she would have to tell him—to give him the choice of being in their daughter's life.

Her brother, Daniel, had left her and Maria high and dry, and while for her sister the betrayal had meant that the charity she worked so hard for had come to the brink of collapse, it had hit Celine differently. She too had fond feelings for the charity, but it wasn't what she spent most of her time working on. No, Daniel leaving had left their relationship shredded to ribbons—a bond between the two siblings that had previously been ironclad. Or at least she'd thought that until the moment he had dumped Mirabel at this house and left to run after his mistress.

The situation had been hauntingly similar

to the one with Darius, where she had tried calling, sending texts and asking friends to deliver messages if they ever saw him. Just to get some closure.

But she had to admit to herself that she had never been important enough to either of them to be accorded that respect. Even now, Darius was only here because he needed to defer their divorce, that she had been waiting too long to file—putting her life on pause for a man she wasn't even sure she wanted any more.

A ragged breath left Darius's mouth, then another as he looked around the room, his eyes snagging on the subtle details around them— indications that a child lived here with her.

'You…' He paused, staring towards the door, where Celine spotted some of Nina's shoes stacked next to her own. 'I…have a daughter?'

An avalanche of emotions rippled across his face. Too many for Celine to pinpoint exactly what was going on in his head. He probably didn't know either. How was he supposed to react to the news of the child they had made together?

She swallowed, considering her next words. Though, from where she was standing, she felt justified in laying the blame at his feet, she didn't want to overwhelm him with that now, when he was processing a far more important piece of information.

'You do. I tried to get in touch with you in every way possible. But when calls and texts went unanswered I assumed you weren't interested in me or her.' This time she could identify the emotion in his expression—shame.

That took her by surprise. She had expected anger towards her, or the indifference she'd believed he felt when he hadn't replied to her messages. Celine had prepared herself for those, steeled her will against the blame she'd believed he would hurl at her.

But his expression was one of shock…and guilt.

'*Dios…*' he whispered as he scrubbed his hands over his face, threading his fingers through his short hair.

Celine wanted to give him some space to process everything and sort through his thoughts, but she needed to get this off her chest too. The effort to speak up about this after so long had her trembling and if she didn't say everything at once she feared they would have to repeat the same conversation many times over.

'I'm willing to give you the time you need, and I want to offer you something more. A choice.' She paused to take a breath as Darius's wary eyes darted back to her. 'I'm telling you all of this because I want Nina to know her father. I *want* you in her life—I've always wanted that. But if you want to be a part of her life, you need to be in it for good. If you can't promise that, then leave and send me the papers when you're done. If you do—'

Darius shot up from his chair, his hand pressed flat onto the table between them and his expression thunderous. 'You don't need to finish your sentence. There is no way I'm walking away from my daughter when I already missed so much of her life...'

There was a pause—an incomplete sentence that Celine really wanted him to finish. The information omitted—the *why* around missing the first five years of his child's life—had tormented her for just as long.

Pushing those overwhelming thoughts away, she forced herself to nod. 'Okay, that's good. Then we have an agreement. You can meet Nina, and we'll tell her you're her father.'

Darius blanched, something she understood well as an icy chill pooled in the pit of her stomach. She knew her daughter well, knew that the question of where her father was had been on her mind, even at such a young age.

'What does she know about me?' he asked, picking up her strand of thought.

It almost made her smile how he could still guess her thoughts by the expression on her face alone. When they had been together, their non-verbal communication had been good enough to have entire conversations without saying a word.

'She knows she has a father and that he's been away.' Celine chose her words carefully, both now and whenever she spoke to Nina about her absent father. 'Whenever she had questions about you, I tried to answer them to my best ability without assigning any blame. Regardless of what you did to me, I never made her aware of my feelings about you.'

Darius started pacing in the small kitchen, his eyes darting around as he processed the magnitude of the news she had shared with him. Though she couldn't really blame him, the constant steps were ratcheting up her own nerves.

Being near him was bringing back so many feelings from the past that Celine fought hard to push them back down into the pit they had crawled out of. She couldn't afford to think about Darius the way she used to, *especially* not if he was about to become a constant in her life—her daughter's life—again.

The hurt of his abandonment still burned beneath her skin. Or was the heat coming from somewhere else—somewhere she didn't dare to look at?

'Do you want to see a photo of her?' she blurted out to distract herself from the torrent of emotions bubbling up in her chest.

Darius froze mid-stride, turning his head towards her with wide eyes that showed a mixture of longing and shock. The latter she could understand all too well, but it was the rawness of the former that made her heart skip a beat. He *really* was excited to know more about her. Had he already embraced the instant bond of parenthood that had sprung to life when she had revealed the news about Nina to him?

Celine grabbed her phone off the table and opened her camera roll to the latest photos of Nina, taken last weekend at Mirabel's birthday party, where she had insisted on dressing up like an extravagant princess and promptly dropped a slice of cake onto her puffy dress. Though instead of crying, as Celine had expected, Nina had simply dusted herself off and continued eating with a raised chin.

Her estranged husband stepped closer as she turned the phone around for him to see the image, then grabbed it with a soft reverence, as if he were handling Nina herself. He fell back onto the chair, as if his legs could no longer carry him.

'She is...*preciosa*,' he breathed, and the awe lacing his voice made her smile.

'She is very lovely, yes,' she replied, and the smile spreading over his lips when he looked up at her was so full of warmth and love that her breath caught in her throat as her heart sped up.

'When can I meet her?' he asked, bringing up the question Celine didn't have an answer to, because how did one set up a meeting between a long-estranged father and a daughter he never knew he had?

Celine searched within herself for an answer to the question she'd asked herself all day. She didn't know what to do about them meeting. Because she genuinely wanted the two to get to know each other, but every time she imagined it her heart stopped with fear of the inevitable fallout. What if he didn't stay true to his word and left again? She couldn't stand Nina suffering the same abandonment her cousin Mirabel had.

Yet even though Daniel had failed to appear in her life again, Celine could see how happy her niece was despite all that had happened to her. Maria had become a new mother to her, Rafael stepping into the father role for both her and Nina. They had forged their own happy ending, with both Dias sisters and Mirabel accepting reality for what it was and taking the bad with the good.

'How do I know you won't leave again?' she asked, wanting to hear the words so she could remind him of them if things went wrong.

He lifted his head to meet her probing gaze. 'I promise you I want to be a part of her life and I will never abandon her.'

'Your promises haven't meant much in the past,' Celine said, suppressing a wince when his expression crumpled.

'My word is all I have to offer, Celine.' She watched as his hand scrubbed over his face, a heavy sigh dropping from his lips. Celine knew she would let him meet Nina, *wanted* it even. But that didn't mean the protectiveness within her was easily overcome. It didn't change that she'd had to go through the birth on her own. The long nights that had followed the equally long days leading up to Nina's first birthday that she had had to struggle through by herself, feeding her child while also working to keep a roof over their heads.

Celine couldn't have done it without her sister, but it should have been Darius who shared the burden with her.

She had to remind herself that it wasn't about her feelings for him, but rather Nina getting to know her father. Even if he didn't stand by his commitment to be her father, they would be fine. They had been so far, and they would find a way to heal again. The reward of Nina having her father in her life for ever was worth the risk of it going bad. Rip it off like a plaster, she told herself. Nothing she could do would prepare Nina for this meeting, so she might as well dive in headfirst.

'I asked Maria to take her for a few hours so we could talk in private,' she said, then she took her phone out of Darius's hands. 'I'll text her and let her know she can bring her back now.'

Darius's nerves were jangling, each sensation magnified to such an extent that he wasn't sure he would ever feel normal again. His thoughts were racing, everything inside of him reeling at the news Celine had dropped on him out of nowhere.

He was a father. Nearly six years ago, on their wedding night, they had made a child. Nina.

When Darius had come here to ask for his estranged wife's help, this hadn't been on the cards at all. A child? With Celine? There had been a time when that had been his dearest wish, wanting nothing else than to grow a family with her. Now it was this tension-filled moment as he sat opposite the woman he had married six years ago, who was staring daggers at him from across the table.

Darius wanted to be angry with her, and a part of him believed himself betrayed out of the first five years of his daughter's life, years filled with importance and influence that she'd had to live without him—that *he'd* had to live without knowing *her.* But he couldn't let the fury bubbling in his veins show. Not when he had only himself to blame.

He had made the choice to stay in Peru, to not follow through with their plan of getting a spouse visa so he could return to Brazil. When he had told his mother that he was going back to Brazil to be with Celine, she had revealed the severity of her sickness—along with the debt she had incurred in Brazil trying to save her failing business. She had told him she wanted him to be a part of Delgado Cosmetics, even though he'd shown no interest in it.

But when she'd revealed what kind of people she had borrowed money from—the threats they were sending her—he knew he had to help her, especially because the cancer was progressing so fast. How could he have turned away when she had done so much for him?

Leona Delgado had lifted herself out of poverty so she could give Darius a good life. What had started out as a small stall in a weekly farmers' market in Manaus where she sold homemade skincare and make-up products had become a skincare company that was known for its high quality and humble beginnings right in their kitchen.

From there, his mother had reached for more, worked harder than anyone to bring them out of poverty and into a place where she could pay for his education and give him a better life than she'd had.

It was only after her death that he'd discovered her deception—that the threat to him and his wife didn't exist. That he hadn't had to stay away to keep Celine safe... To think that he could have returned then, explained himself and asked for her forgiveness... He would have had an extra year with his daughter, one more birthday that had come and gone without her knowing him.

The decision not to get in touch with Celine after he'd learned the extent of his mother's lies sat in the pit of his stomach like an ice-coated boulder. He had wanted to, but whenever his hand gravitated towards his phone he'd stopped and examined his feelings. Wanting to reach out just to explain his side of things wasn't a good enough reason—it needed to be more than just him trying to rid himself of the guilt he carried around.

But he'd suspected she had moved on, that she had found someone far more worthy of her affection than him. His selfishness had inflicted enough pain in her life—so he'd chosen to stay away for good. Until the divorce papers had arrived, opening a door that couldn't be closed any more. They would be in each other's lives until their last days.

The phone on the table vibrated and his heart skipped a beat when Celine grabbed it, reading the message she'd received.

'She says they're finishing up lunch and then she'll bring her over. Won't be longer than half an hour,' she said, her voice wavering.

His pulse rate raised, and he forced himself to breathe. He didn't know the first thing about being a father—or what to expect from his daughter. He swallowed the lump of anxiety forming in his throat, then he said, 'Can you tell me more about Nina? What is she like?'

Darius prepared himself to be laughed at, as he wasn't sure this question even made sense. She was five, after all. The realisation of how little experience he had with children flooded his stomach with dread. Would Nina realise he had no idea what it meant to be a parent and reject him for his clumsy attempts?

But Celine didn't laugh. She turned a thoughtful gaze towards him, and the smile that spread over her face was so gentle and warm he forgot to breathe for a few heartbeats.

'She's the best. Her current obsession is dinosaurs, so everything needs to involve dinosaurs somehow. She's about to start school next February, and even though that's still more than half a year away, she is so keen that she's already picked out her school bag and pencil case and everything.' Celine paused with a smirk. 'All also covered in dinosaurs, so I hope this particular interest lasts her a while.'

Celine's phone vibrated again, and his stomach dropped when she said, 'She's outside.'

She got up and strode towards the door, her hand stopping on top of the door handle as she hesitated. Darius's heart was pounding so hard he was worried it would escape his chest.

'You're sure about this?' he forced himself to ask, even though he didn't want her to reconsider.

She gave a short laugh. 'No, but I know that has everything to do with me and not her.' Celine threw him a look over her shoulder. 'She deserves to know her dad. My personal feelings don't matter.'

And with that Celine opened the door. A smile immediately spread over her face, and she crouched down, opening her arms. *'Oi, filha,'* he heard her say, and then a small figure stepped into Celine's open arms, throwing her slender arms around her neck.

Darius held his breath as he looked at his daughter, the onslaught of emotions too much for him to process. The moment Celine had told him about Nina a bond sprang to life within him that now firmed into a solid attachment of affection and the need to protect her.

Her hair was the same dark brown as Celine's and tied up in a bun on each side of her head, and she was wearing a grey shirt with a little T-Rex printed on it. But when she turned her head he took in a sharp breath as his own brown eyes stared at him.

'We have a visitor here today,' Celine said in a quiet voice, wrapping her hands around their daughter's arms and pushing her away so she could look at her. 'Remember when I told you that your father lives in a different country and that's why he's not here?'

Her voice was gentle and there was no accusation there, yet her words hit him like a punch in the gut. She had been forced to have this conversation with their daughter when he hadn't even known that she existed. He pushed the anger down, not wanting Nina to see anything about his inner thoughts on his face. There was already some reluctance in her stance.

Nina only nodded, her eyes darting between Celine and him.

'Well, he's finally back in Brazil and he's come over to meet you. Would you be okay with that?'

Nina remained quiet, her gaze now focused on Darius as she scanned him, an understanding in her eyes that he would have thought to be beyond the comprehension of a five-year-old child. He didn't know what to do. Was he supposed to go over and say hello? Stay where he was and let her approach him?

Celine made that decision for him when she got up, her hand wrapped around Nina's. She looked at the door, giving a short nod, then closed it before taking a step back towards him.

Nina immediately stepped behind her mother, hiding behind her legs and peering at Darius with a wary expression. His heart was racing, so were his thoughts as he struggled to come up with something—*anything*—to say that would have meaning. Words that would soothe the years he'd spent not knowing she existed. That would show her and Celine how much this moment meant to him. How sorry he was.

'Do you want to say hello to your father, Nina?' Celine asked, looking over her shoulder down to her daughter, who was clinging to her leg with fierce little hands.

Her eyes were as round as saucers, then she squeezed them shut and shook her head. 'Uh-uh,' he heard her say, her grip on her mother's trousers so tight that her knuckles were turning white.

Celine clicked her tongue with a shake of her head, her hand resting on Nina's head and patting her. 'Are you sure? He came a long way to see you.'

Nina shook her head even more furiously, and the pressure in his chest built so much that he felt his heart crack. Her reluctance was understandable since he was no more than a stranger to her, but that didn't make it any easier to deal with.

'Okay, you don't have to.' Celine got on her haunches again, looking at Nina. 'Why don't you go up and get ready for a nap? I'll be with you in a moment.'

Darius watched with mixed feelings as Nina—his daughter—turned away from him with wide eyes and then scurried out of view and up the stairs.

Celine looked after her with a sigh, then shook her head before addressing him. 'We'll try again tomorrow. She wasn't expecting that and just needs some time to process.'

She grabbed her phone and held it out to him. 'Give me your number, and I'll text you the details for tomorrow. Might be easier on her if we go somewhere she likes, so she feels more at ease.'

Darius nodded, typing his number into her phone, and then stood up with the heaviness of a hundred boulders falling into the pit of his stomach. How was he going to win Nina over when he knew nothing about her or being a father?

The dark cloud these thoughts caused followed him as he bade Celine goodnight and made his way back to his hotel two towns over.

CHAPTER FIVE

OVER THE NEXT WEEK Nina slowly warmed to the idea of having her dad in her life and it made Celine breathe easier. In retrospect, she thought she might have handled the initial meeting better and given her daughter more forewarning of who she was about to meet. Though Darius had put on a brave face when he'd left, she could tell he'd been crushed by Nina's reaction.

But now, a week after Darius's sudden reappearance and his introduction to their daughter, Nina was daring to get closer to him and showing more interest in him. The concept of a father was still new for her, having only ever experienced it second-hand through encounters with her friends' families.

Today they had decided to go to the weekly farmers' market held in Santarém's town square—on the urging of Maria. She and Rafael enjoyed diving into the different stalls that came to the town, sampling every single thing and talking to everyone about the latest gossip.

Celine had never felt the same connection to the town and its people the way Maria did, and she understood why. Her sister was more sociable, attending all of the town meetings and keeping them informed about the happenings in town. She also spent way more time maintaining their home and spent more time put. Celine was more on the road than she was at home, as her patients needed her to go to them. Unlike Maria, the people she had bonded with were the farmers she worked with. Like Juliana and her wife, who had jumped at the opportunity to get rid of all their toddler gear once they'd got close enough to hear about Celine's situation.

She let her eyes drift in search of the familiar blonde hair but couldn't detect her in the crowd. Since the farms were in remote locations, many of her clients would come to Santarém on weekends to enjoy some time away from work.

'You want a hot chocolate? In this weather?' Darius's voice filtered over to her, and she watched with a small smile as he bent down to Nina, who nodded enthusiastically.

'It's never too warm for hot chocolate,' she replied with a grin that melted Celine's heart.

Watching the two interact with each other was a lot more heart-warming than she'd thought it would be—and it tied the knot of complex feelings towards Darius even tighter. The largest part of her was still angry at him, furious that he had left, that he had never answered a single phone call or text message.

But beneath the surface was an ever-increasing heat bubbling up inside of her. Each time she caught the tendrils of warmth—flashes of attraction and longing—she forced them back down into non-existence. The attraction had clicked back into place the moment they had sat in her truck together, with his scent mingling in her space and his smile bringing a wobble to her knees. His faults notwithstanding, the man she had married was still remarkable and stupidly handsome, to the point where she cursed him for it. Letting Darius back into her life was one thing but being attracted to her soon-to-be ex-husband was a complication Celine didn't need. No, it had been too easy for him to abandon her, and one week was not enough to prove himself worthy.

She pushed the thoughts away when the pair came strolling back to the picnic bench she sat on. Darius sat down opposite her, and Nina, to her surprise, slipped into the space next to her father.

He set down a cup in front of her that Celine eyed suspiciously. The walk from her house to the town square had been quiet and pleasant, feeling reminiscent of a time when they had loved nothing more than to spend time with each other. It had been like Celine had slipped into a vision of what her life would have looked like if they had stayed together, had raised Nina together and planned their weekends like a real family would. Like Maria and Rafael did…

The thought had freaked her out so much she'd needed some distance from Darius, so she had sent him with Nina to Emanuel's stand to get them a beverage.

'What is this?' she asked as she grabbed the cup. It was warm, and the scent of coffee wiggled its way through the closed plastic lid and up her nose—along with another, more subtle fragrance.

'It's a cappuccino but, instead of cocoa powder, I asked them to put on a sprinkling of cinnamon.' He flashed her a grin when her eyes widened. 'Ah, so you still like it? I wasn't sure and this little one says Tia Maria is not impressed with your coffee.'

Celine's eyes darted to Nina. 'Your *tia* said she doesn't like my coffee? Is that true?'

Nina giggled into her hot chocolate, amused

by her mother's faux outrage. 'She says it tastes like dirty water.'

'Nina!'

Darius laughed, the rumble of his voice so deep and clear that it floated through the air between them, vibrating through her skin and settling into the pit of her stomach—which was already performing loops from being so close to her estranged husband and the unwanted attraction rearing its head.

'Well, I think what—'

Nina's delighted squeal interrupted whatever Darius had been about to say, and she waved her hand at someone behind Celine. Both her parents looked over, and Celine locked eyes with her sister just as Nina threw her tiny arms around Mirabel. Despite their age difference, the cousins had grown accustomed to each other's company when she and Maria had lived together in the small house she now occupied with Nina.

'Well, that's her gone for the rest of the afternoon,' she said and couldn't stop a groan dropping from her lips.

Darius raised his eyebrows. 'What's wrong?'

'I should have figured Maria would come here today. Now she's going to think all sorts of nonsense because she saw us together.'

'But she's also seen me come to your house

this week,' he said. 'What's different about today?'

Celine snorted as she considered her answer. A part of her didn't want to go into any details. Not with him, not when he had hurt her so much that the memory alone pushed the air out of her lungs. But the constant fight against her attraction for Darius was wearing her down, the restraints easing as the days went by. The part of her that remembered what his arms felt like around her yearned for one last taste. Especially when those arms had only grown stronger in the past six years, she thought as her eyes took in the muscles peeking out of his T-shirt.

There was no chance of a reunion for them, she already knew that. There were too many open questions for her to be comfortable with him, but daydreaming didn't ever hurt anyone, right?

'They had their big romantic moment here at the farmers' market, where they presented themselves to the entire village as a couple,' she said, pushing the unwanted thoughts aside to focus on their conversation. Better she shared this little titbit rather than voice the other things popping into her head.

Celine wasn't going to rehash any of his past mistakes with Darius. Not only was it necessary for them to have a cordial co-parenting relationship, she also simply didn't want to know. There was no way he could say anything that would make her forgive him.

Celine had moved on with her life, from the idea of being married to Darius—she wanted the real deal. And that wasn't going to be Darius again. Not when he had trusted her so little that he couldn't even tell her his mother had been sick.

No, there was more behind his disappearance than he let on. Instead of coming clean, Darius was choosing to keep more secrets from her. Celine tried not to care. If they had been truly meant for each other, then things would have happened differently all those years ago. He would have trusted her.

But he hadn't, and Celine found the longer she thought about it, the less she wanted to know why—or the cage around her memories and feelings for him might grow even weaker, leaving her exposed and broken once more. If she had learned anything from being married in name only for six years and then watching Maria struggle through issues with Rafael, it was that someone who truly loved her would have stayed with her—or at least told her the truth.

Darius hadn't done either, and she needed

to remind herself of that more often. Because the smile that lit up his face as his eyes drifted towards her daughter melted her heart so much it fell out of its beat. The scene that she had dreamt about for so long had suddenly appeared in front of her, but it was all wrong. The trust was gone, no matter how enticing the picture he now painted was to her.

'She had to introduce her husband to the entire village?' His voice had an incredulous edge that Celine understood far better than he would ever realise.

'Well…kind of? Santarém is so small, there aren't even a thousand people living here. That means everyone becomes *família*, and if someone new wants to join, they have to prove themselves.'

Darius nodded, his eyes darting over to Emanuel's stall. 'That explains the frosty look I received from that guy.'

'Did he give you grief?' Celine's eyes narrowed on the coffee shop owner, who was too busy serving his next customers to notice anything.

'You don't sound so appreciative of that,' he replied.

Her eyes snapped back to him at his words, rounding at the huskiness she heard in his voice. 'Maria loves them, but I prefer for people to stay out of my business.'

'You're not close to the villagers, then?'

The question gave her pause, for it highlighted a truth within her that everyone else around her seemed to be aware of, but nobody really wanted to address. Yet it had taken Darius one interaction to see through the complex web of relationships that kept this town going.

'Maria spends a lot more time at the clinic and with the people of Santarém. My job has me driving around to farms all week, so by default I don't get to spend a lot of time around them. I'm far closer to people like Juliana because I see them more often than the villagers,' she said, hinting at the obvious answer to the far more complex question of how she felt about Santarém.

Because the truth was something that she closely guarded—that she had come here out of necessity more than desire, and that she missed living in Manaus. A part of her wanted to leave and pick up the city life again, but not only would she be uprooting Nina's life, she also owed her sister too much to just leave now that everything was more stable. Maria had dropped everything to help her when Nina had been born, spending nights with her so that Celine could get some sleep. Though her role in the clinic had diminished since Rafael had arrived, she couldn't abandon her sister's dream when Maria had saved her in her time of need. There was a debt she needed to pay back and she would not abandon her duties as a sister for some misguided ideas about the freedom of city life.

'I see,' Darius replied in a tone that she knew far too well and that hadn't changed in the last six years. He knew her answer was evasive—but he wasn't supposed to know that.

She didn't have time to come up with a retort as he said, 'You came here because you needed help, and I wasn't around any more.'

Celine started at the sudden vulnerability in his expression, at the admission of guilt that she saw in his features. Over the last week she had sensed regret in some of his words, but none had been so evident as what he had just said.

'I…' Her voice trailed off as she tried to find the right words to say. His behaviour in the last week had not at all been what she had expected. She'd thought he would justify his absence, find excuses and argue with her. Enough time had passed for her to replace the loving and kind image she had of Darius with one built from hurt and anger over his abandonment of her, of the daughter he had never known.

But now her heart was softening as she saw the version of her husband that she had fallen in love with all those years ago.

'Yes, I came here because I didn't want to be alone. But now that she's older I—'

The clattering of plates interrupted her, followed by a loud shriek laced with terror.

'Álvaro!' The shouts came from where the food stalls stood, and Darius scanned the crowd that was forming around a man lying prone on the ground. A woman was kneeling next to him, and another woman sat on the ground, slumped against a food truck.

Darius surged to his feet, the conversation with Celine all but forgotten in the face of the medical emergency. He pushed some onlookers aside, then knelt next to the man named Álvaro. His face was a ghostly white, his hands and legs twitching involuntarily, his eyes closed but moving back and forth under his lids. Behind him Darius heard the soft moans and hisses from the other woman. Did they have some altercation? He looked back at the man in front of him. There were no obvious marks of an injury, but rather the signs of a seizure.

'What are you doing?' A middle-aged woman looked at him with confusion, and from the frantic look in her eyes he guessed she must be related to the patient—but he didn't have time to contemplate that. Not while Álvaro was having a seizure. He quickly glanced at the watch on his wrist, memorising the minutes and seconds so he could time the seizure.

'It's okay, Magda. He is a doctor.' Celine's voice drifted towards him, and he looked up. 'Did anyone already call emergency services?' she asked, looking at him.

Darius looked at his watch again, then up. 'If the seizure lasts less than five minutes, we don't need to declare it an emergency.'

He moved to the other side of the patient and pushed the man onto his side, pulling his arm underneath him at an angle that would ensure Álvaro wouldn't hurt himself while having a seizure. When he had ensured that the patient was in the recovery position, he got to his feet again.

'Does he have any existing condition that cause seizures?' he asked, looking at Magda, who shook her head as a sob escaped her throat.

'No, nothing of the sort. He has diabetes but never anything like this,' the old woman replied, kneeling on the ground next to her husband. 'What's wrong with him?'

Darius frowned as he crouched down as well to be eye to eye with Magda as he explained. 'See the twitching of his arms and legs? That's most likely because he's having a grand mal seizure. It comes in different stages. One of them is the slackening of muscles followed by tensing, as you can see here. The first symptom is usually a change that we call aura. Did Álvaro complain about sensing something strange? A smell or a taste that was agitating him?'

Magda's eyes rounded as she listened to his explanation and then she looked down, both of her hands resting on Álvaro's side. 'He didn't enjoy the coffee we got at Emanuel's, which is strange because that is his favourite part of the farmers' market. Just now we got his soup, and that's when it started. He threw the soup at poor Bruna while she was cutting up my sandwich…'

She looked over her shoulder to the woman slumped against the wheel of the food truck, a pained expression on her face. When his eyes dipped below to where one hand was clutching her arm, he noticed the cloth Bruna was pressing against her forearm that was slowly turning red.

Darius looked up and caught Celine's eyes on him. A pang of heat sliced through his chest at the concern etched into her features and he pushed it away. Now was not the time.

'It's been almost a minute since Álvaro went down. Can you alert me when five minutes have passed? I must check on Bruna over here.' Magda nodded, and he turned to look at the woman's injury. He crouched down in front of her and she opened her eyes when she felt his hand on her shoulder. 'Bruna, I'm Dr Delgado. Can I have a look at that wound?'

Bruna nodded, and Darius noted her pain-glazed eyes as her eyelids fluttered open and closed again. With delicate hands he prised Bruna's fingers away from her arm, then unwrapped the cloth. He swallowed the hiss rising in his throat, needing to project calmness so his patient wouldn't panic at any outward sign.

'I have to inspect the cut. This will be uncomfortable and I'm sorry for that,' he said to prepare her for his probing fingers.

The cut went along the upper side of her arm, he noted with relief. Though it was long, it wasn't deep and a few stitches would see Bruna as good as new. Had the cut been on the other side, it might have hit the radial artery and caused far more blood loss than presented here.

'I have good news for you. Though painful, this cut is shallow, and it avoided any major blood vessels. We'll be able to stitch you up here if I can find everything I'm looking for. Do you have any fresh towels in your truck that we can use to staunch the bleeding while I look for the first aid kit?'

Bruna opened her mouth but a low voice from behind interrupted her. 'Take this,' Emanuel, the coffee shop owner, said as he handed Darius a fresh hand towel that he carefully draped around the wound and pressed down on it for a few moments. The bleeding would not stop on its own, the gash too wide to knit itself back together, so until he could stitch it they needed to apply constant pressure.

He looked at Emanuel with a grateful smile. 'Can you keep pressure on the wound while I look at Álvaro?' The man nodded, then took Bruna's arm between his two hands and pressed down on the makeshift bandaging.

When Darius raised his head he saw Celine kneeling beside Magda, who whispered encouragement into her husband's ear. He glanced at his watch—three minutes and twenty-three seconds—then at Álvaro. The muscle spasms were less pronounced now, the rapid movements of his eyes gone, and when Darius reached out to feel his pulse it was slowing down—along with his breathing. Then Álvaro's mouth fell open, releasing a sigh that Darius felt in the depth of his bones.

'Magda,' he called out to get the attention of the old woman. 'The seizure is over, and Álvaro should wake up in a few moments. He might not remember that he had a seizure, and he will definitely be confused. It's best that you take him home to rest. Once he feels a bit more stable, you should call your general practitioner and discuss what happened. Your doctor will refer him to the right specialist for treatment. Did you come here by car?'

Darius looked around. They had walked here, and he hadn't seen any cars parked along the side of the road. Santarém was so small, he didn't think anyone would ever bother to drive here. Confirming his suspicion, Magda shook her head.

'We live just down the road from here,' she said, pointing at the principal road that wound itself alongside the town square.

Darius looked at Celine with a frown. 'I would drive them, but I have to take care of Bruna. She needs stitches for the cut on her arm.'

'Rafael will drive them home. He already

left to fetch his car.' A familiar voice drifted towards his ears, and Maria appeared in front of them. She had her arm wrapped around the shoulder of an older girl—her niece Mirabel—and held onto his daughter's hand with her other one.

Darius's eyes rounded as a lump appeared in his throat. He'd been expecting to come face to face with Maria eventually and had steeled himself for whatever she would hurl at him. During the early days of his and Celine's budding relationship her sister had been fiercely protective of her, scrutinising his intentions on more than one occasion.

Whatever she had to say to him would have to wait for another time. With Álvaro's taxi sorted, he had to find everything he needed to stitch a wound, along with a sterile environment. He couldn't perform any medical procedure out here in the open.

'Do you have a local GP here?' he asked, hoping a fellow medical doctor would help him out in this situation.

But Celine shook her head. 'The GP is one village over.'

The sigh building in Darius's chest caught in his throat when an idea dawned on him. He didn't need to be in a *medical* practice. A cut on a human was surely treated similarly to a cut in a different mammal. 'You have iodine solution, sterile needles, forceps and thread in your clinic?'

Celine's eyes rounded when she followed his request. 'You want to stitch her up in the clinic?'

'It's mostly the same process. Do you use nylon sutures?'

She nodded, then got to her feet. 'I'll go ahead and prep a room. Can you and Emanuel see if Bruna is strong enough to walk?'

Darius nodded, then squatted back down as Nina approached them, opening his arms to give the girl a quick hug and a kiss on her forehead. 'I'm not going to be long, my sweet,' he said to her with a smile as she scurried back behind her aunt's legs.

Darius wished he had the time to look around and take in the clinic as a whole. Throughout their relationship he had heard so much about the animal charity that the Dias family ran here on the edge of the rainforest. But he couldn't take even a moment for himself when his patient was still in pain and losing blood.

Celine awaited him at the front door, ushering him through the reception and into one of the back rooms. As he stepped through the door, he already noticed all the necessary equipment laid out in a portable tray—gloves, sutures, vacuum-sealed needles and forceps, a bottle of iodine solution and the roll of bandages. He almost had to laugh as he looked at the assortment of tools.

'You had all of this already?' he asked, looking at Celine.

She nodded. 'Yeah, Maria uses all of this in her work every day. I don't really get to do a lot of stitching on the farms. Livestock usually don't cut themselves very often, and if they do, the farmers are well equipped to take care of that themselves.'

'Our work isn't really that different,' he said, then he sat on the stool next to Bruna, pulling the gloves on his hands. 'The only thing we can't do here is numb your skin before we stitch it. Unfortunately, the medication animals and humans use is different in that regard. But we have given you some pain meds. They won't help with the immediate pain, but they will take the edge off once you rest. I will try to be as fast and precise as possible, okay?'

Bruna nodded, and then winced when he unwrapped the hand towel that had soaked up quite a bit of blood on the way to the clinic. He held out the towel in an almost automatic gesture, being used to having an assistant helping him with any procedures the players on the team went through. But before he could get up to dispose of the towel himself, Celine grabbed it and threw it in a bin marked as a biohazardous waste.

Darius nodded, grateful for her assistance, then grabbed the sponge lying in the shallow bowl on the tray and cleaned the area around the cut. Bruna winced again, but held still as he continued and washed away all of the debris. As he prepped the needle and sutures, popping the forceps out of their sterile packaging and threading the nylon, Celine's hand appeared on Bruna's shoulder to give it a reassuring squeeze.

'Okay, I'm going to start now.' Her breath left her body in shaking trembles as Darius poked the needle through the skin then gathered both sides of the cut to align them for suturing.

To help her with the pain, he worked as fast as he dared without compromising the quality of his work—something that was harder said than done. Though he had trained in a hospital and done countless sutures in his time there, it had been a few years since he'd had to stitch someone up. Though his football players lived a dangerous life on the pitch, their injuries were often torn muscles and ligaments, not knife wounds.

As he focused on the stitches, Celine said softly, 'You're doing great. We're more than halfway through with the sutures. A bit more and then you can go home. Rafael is already waiting to take you.'

Warmth pooled in the pit of his stomach, radiating through his body in gentle tendrils as he listened to his wife as she calmed Bruna. In the first years of their relationship he had often fantasised about what it would be like to work together. Though their patients were vastly different, the empathy and diligence they needed to show them remained the same.

'Can you hand me the bandages?' he asked, then started wrapping the freshly stitched wound after brushing it with some iodine solution to keep any infection at bay.

He gently tapped Bruna's arm when he was done, drawing her gaze towards him. 'Okay, we are all done here. This should heal just fine, but since we used nylon sutures you need to have them removed. I suggest you get in contact with your GP and schedule an appointment so they can have a look at it.'

Bruna looked at him with wide eyes. 'You're not going to be here?'

'No, I'm just visiting,' he said with a shake of his head.

A knock sounded, and Rafael poked his head into the exam room. 'We're all set here?'

Celine nodded, then helped Bruna off her chair and ushered her through the door and into the care of Rafael.

Silence settled between them that was only interrupted by Celine shuffling the used equipment around. Darius cleared his throat as tension rose in his body.

'Thanks for setting all of this up,' he said, then took a step forward and handed her the things on the tray.

Celine gave a quiet laugh and when she looked back at him his breath caught in his throat at the sight of her. Her eyes were gentle, filled with an emotion that he couldn't quite pinpoint. All he knew was that the apprehension he'd seen was gone, melted away and replaced by something warm. Affection? Or was that what he wanted to see?

'I have to give thanks. I don't know what we would have done without you today.' She hesitated, flipping the used forceps in her hand, then she continued. 'I was impressed with your quick thinking and your care for Bruna and Alvaro. Seeing you work was…nice.'

His heart accelerated at her words, and without conscious input he took a step forward. The warm tendrils that had been sweeping across his body intensified, flaring to life in a blaze that set his blood to a boil.

He wanted to touch her so badly, wanted to press her against the wall and cover her body with his. The last few days had not only shown him how much of his daughter's life he had missed, but also how much of their married life had slipped through his fingers.

Celine watched him with wary eyes as he stepped closer, though something was different about her stance. The high walls he'd sensed around her in every interaction they'd had this week—they seemed lower. All because she'd watched him help the villagers? Any doctor would have done the same as him.

He hadn't seen that side of her ever since he had come back into her life a week ago, and it was so mesmerising that he forgot where he was—forgot what kind of relationship they had now, where the touches he'd once shared with her were now inconceivable. Instinct—or habit, Darius wasn't too sure—took possession of his motor functions as he leaned forward and kissed her on the cheek.

His hand settled down on her hip for a fraction of a second, then he stepped back, fishing his car keys out of his pocket. 'I have to go check on Álvaro. But I'll see you at your place?'

* * *

'I'll see you at your place.'

Celine hadn't registered his departing words, too stunned by the sudden kiss he had given her on her cheek—and what that small gesture had done to her.

A cascade of heat had rippled through her body, starting at her cheeks and tumbling all the way down to her stomach, where it settled in her core. Even now, as she sat on her couch and watched Nina flip through a book illustrating all the wild animals of the rainforest, she felt a tingle where his lips had brushed her skin.

An unwanted and unbidden reaction to what had no doubt been an innocent gesture that Darius hadn't thought through. That it rattled her to her very core was a problem Celine needed to examine on her own, not daring to speak to anyone about how the touch had made her heart beat faster—how that traitorous voice inside her was calling for more.

This could not be happening. These…feelings could not re-emerge from the place she had banished them to when Darius had decided not to come back to her. Six years ago, she had taken the love for her husband—the emotions that had been shredding her insides with the grief of his abandonment—and had put them in a locked box so she could move on with her life.

Now he was back, and not only was his scent alluring and his lips as soft as she remembered, he had also slotted into her life almost as seamlessly as if he had belonged with her all this time. The picture of the family she had wanted them to be, had dreamed of as they'd got married in a rush, was the reality that was unfolding in front of Celine now. Watching him work had only reaffirmed the thoughts in her head. His compassion and care for Bruna and Álvaro had touched a part inside of her that had remained dormant ever since he had walked out on her.

Celine had to admit that she had held onto the idea of her marriage miraculously mending itself for far too long, unwilling to admit that the family she had dreamt of when they had fallen in love was nothing more than an idle dream of a foolish woman in love.

When Maria had found love with Rafael, Celine realised she had been holding onto nothing but a figment of her dream. A made-up lie she had been clinging onto because she hadn't wanted to admit that she had married a man who had then betrayed her—a marriage that was holding her back from finding the one person who would be hers unquestioningly, the way Rafael belonged to Maria.

Darius was not this person. He couldn't be, despite his undeniable allure, bringing her back into his orbit. When he had elected not to return, he had irrevocably shattered Celine's trusting nature and the scepticism that had sprung to life had her rejecting any kind of closeness before it could get serious.

A problem she would have to figure out once she met the man who was meant for her. That part of her life would have to wait for another few months until she could finally get divorced and settle into a co-parenting routine with Darius. Right now, she wasn't comfortable leaving him and Nina on their own. But the day would come when she could at least trust him this far, and that day would give her the freedom to pursue other romantic interests.

Now she just needed to douse the fire that sparked to life whenever he was near her. No big deal. Darius meant nothing to her, after all. If he did, she wouldn't be fighting so hard to divorce him.

A knock on the door spooked her out of her thoughts. Celine jumped to her feet and opened the door. Her heart skipped a beat and then resumed its life-giving rhythm with increased speed as she looked into the gorgeous face of her estranged husband, his sculpted jaw and high cheekbones begging her to brush her fingers over them—his mouth twisted in a small smile that she wanted to kiss off his lips.

No big deal at all.

'Hey,' he said, his voice low enough to make her skin tingle. She remembered those deep tones, relishing them whenever he had hummed his desire into her ear as he pushed into her, and she…

'Are you okay? Will you let me in?' Darius's voice drifted through the memory surfacing in her mind, setting off both flames of need and alarm bells within her.

She blinked several times, struggling to chase the vision away, and stepped aside. As he walked past her, his scent crept up her nose, making it so much harder to keep that iron grip on her feelings for this man.

'Um…yeah, of course.' All of her senses were hyperaware of Darius's proximity.

What was happening to her? Darius had left her when she'd needed him the most, when she had agreed to marry him so he could stay in the country. There was too much bad blood between them for her to ever forget that. It didn't matter that he set her heart racing. That didn't change what had happened between them. So how come she couldn't shake these feelings that were re-emerging without her consent?

It was just like Darius to reappear just as she was ready to move on.

'I wasn't sure how long it was going to take you, so I already fed Nina,' Celine said, gesturing towards the dining room table and stepping into the kitchen as he sat down. 'But I have some snacks around, since I'm sure you must be hungry after all of this.'

She didn't wait for a reply, but rather opened the fridge and retrieved a small container with some egg-shaped pastries in it. She fished four of them out, putting them on a plate and shoving them in the microwave.

Her heart was in her throat when she looked at him, the feelings she had been battling rising once more, and the look he gave her made her catch her breath. The same intensity—the same war—was happening in his eyes.

Celine opened her mouth, the tension between them growing as they silently stared at each other, and acted on the need to break the quiet—and hopefully the tension with that. But before she could speak, Darius cleared his throat.

'What is that?' he asked, nodding his chin towards the microwave.

Celine followed his gaze and looked through

the glass of the microwave, watching the food rotate. 'Nina had a little party in kindergarten, so I made some *coxinhas* for it last week.'

A strange expression flitted over Darius's face, one she wasn't able to read, but it set her heart pumping, anyway. Something about it was so soft, so delicate.

'You made *coxinhas*?' he asked, an incredulous edge to his voice.

Celine crossed her arms, leaning her hip against the kitchen counter as she levelled a challenging stare at Darius. 'Don't sound so surprised,' she said, narrowing her eyes at him.

Darius raised his hands in defence. 'I mean no offence, *senhora*. I'm sure I'm simply mis-remembering all the instant ramen that we used to eat at your place.'

She huffed, her lips parting in a reply that was interrupted by the ping of the microwave. Celine stared at him for a moment, then turned around and took the plate out of the micro-wave, setting it in front of him. Then she plopped down on the chair across from him, her eyes darting between him and the plate of food.

'Lucky for you, I had to learn how to feed myself more nutritious things than instant ramen.' Though she framed it as a point of contention, that wasn't actually how she felt about it. During veterinary school, anything that had been cheap and easy had been preferable as she didn't have a lot of time to invest in cooking. Not that she was very good at it. Her mother had gone to the trouble of teaching her the Dias family recipes, and ever since Maria moved out she'd had to learn how to cook rice without burning it. 'Edible' was a compliment in Celine's books.

When she had told her family that she was pregnant, her parents had wanted to defer their retirement in Switzerland, but both Celine and Maria had insisted that they stick to their plans. They had worked tirelessly to support their animal sanctuary, sacrificing holidays, gifts and other luxuries so they could help the animals that couldn't help themselves.

They had come back to Brazil when Nina had been born, meeting their second grandchild after Mirabel, her brother's daughter, who now lived with her sister after Daniel had run away with his mistress to build himself a new life.

Even though she had Maria to lean on, Celine had to figure out so much of motherhood on her own—struggling from mistake to mistake. She would have given anything to have her husband at her side as she'd celebrated Nina's first birthday, or when she had spent sleepless nights as her first teeth grew.

Darius reached for the plate in front of him, taking one of the *coxinhas* into his hand and taking a big bite out of the fried dough ball—a Brazilian speciality her mother had taught her, where they made a savoury chicken filling and stuffed it in a dough that got fried in hot oil for a couple of minutes to give it a crispy golden finish.

Her heart leapt when he closed his eyes, savouring the taste of her food. It was a small gesture, one that shouldn't mean anything to begin with, yet it somehow did.

'How is Álvaro?' she asked to distract herself from the rising desire in her body.

Darius looked at the half-eaten dough ball in his hand. 'He's okay, all things considered. There's no way of telling what caused the seizure. It could be an underlying condition that has just lain dormant within him like epilepsy. Or it could be something more acute, like a tumour or cancer.'

Celine frowned at that. 'Poor Álvaro. He used to run the auto repair shop in town before his son took over just two months ago as he finally retired.' She paused, a smile spreading over her lips despite the bad news for the villager. Watching Darius work with dedication and skill was something she hadn't really experienced in their time together at university.

'We were lucky you were around. Your second chance brought you here and might have saved two lives,' she said before she could consider her words, the underlying meaning not lost on her. Celine shocked herself as she looked inward, finding her words ringing true. Despite her heartache, the missed dreams and broken promises, she was glad he was here with her.

His head snapped up at her words, his eyes locking onto hers as they rounded. 'Second chance? What—'

A shrill beep interrupted his words, and Celine immediately jumped to her feet to reach for her phone on the counter. 'This is my emergency alert. Clients know to send me a message so I get notified day or night. It's foaling season right now, so it's difficult to predict when they might need me.'

Unlocking her screen, she scanned the message, a deep frown on her face. 'The waters on one of Juliana's mares broke ten minutes ago and there's no sign of the foal.'

'Ten minutes? That doesn't seem too long. I thought babies can stay in the birthing canal up to thirty minutes. Is there that much of a difference in horses?' Darius got to his feet as well.

'The time itself is not critical. But because it takes me some time to get there, they know to alert me early. I'd rather drive up and have wasted my time than risk the health of an animal. Especially if it's Juliana asking for my help...' Her mind switched to work mode, looking around the room to find what she needed. Her eyes stopped at Nina. She was thankfully still dressed from her earlier outing, and her overnight bag was leaning against the door, already packed for exactly this sort of situation.

'*Bebê*, please put on your shoes. I have to drop you off at your *tia*'s house because I need to go to work.' Her daughter looked up at her, the drowsiness in her eyes breaking Celine's heart. This situation happened a lot more often than she liked, her need for flexible hours meaning that Nina often needed to go to Maria's place if Celine was called to an emergency. But that usually happened when she hadn't had a full day of activities that left her drained and tired. 'You can have a sleepover with Mirabel,' she added to cheer her up.

Footsteps shuffled behind her, and Celine turned around to see Darius approaching with a hesitant expression on his face that flipped her stomach inside out. Was he going to offer what she thought? She really hoped he didn't, for she didn't know how to have this conversation while sparing his feelings.

'I can watch her if you need to go,' he said, the eagerness in his eyes breaking her heart. He wanted to spend some alone time with his daughter, an idea that both excited and terrified Celine. For the longest time she had been the only parent in Nina's life, and the thought of having another parent now to offload some responsibilities—to lean on when she needed to—was a novel experience that she didn't quite feel comfortable with yet. Just as she wasn't comfortable with the idea of leaving her daughter with the man who had walked out on them.

'Darius…' she began, and the way his eyes shuttered, she knew he understood what she was about to say. 'I just don't feel comfortable with this right now. She has only known you for a week, and I want to give all of us a bit more time before I leave her alone with you.'

Hurt rippled over his expression, and she felt the pain in her own chest as disappointment entered his eyes. Disappointment she could understand very well. One of her favourite things in this world was to hang out with Nina on the couch, watching whatever was on television and holding her close. Those were moments she wanted her daughter to have with her father, but it was still early days and there was a lot of trust to regain before Darius could have these moments with Nina.

Yet still the hurt in his eyes was unbearable, and in an attempt to wipe it away she said, 'Why don't you come to Juliana's farm with me? You were an immense help last time, and depending on how difficult this case is, I could use the extra hands.'

He lifted his brows, clearly surprised by her offer. Hell, her offer surprised *her*. It had slipped out unbidden when the pain in his eyes had become too much for her to withstand. But there was more to it than that, a strange excitement to have him by her side as she worked. A feeling she didn't dare to look at too closely, for she knew that only heartbreak would wait for her at the end of this path.

Despite that though, she smiled when he nodded and stuffed the rest of the dough ball into his mouth.

CHAPTER SIX

THEY ARRIVED AT the farm ten minutes later, with Celine rushing down the empty country road. He had watched as she'd packed her truck with the speedy efficiency of someone who had been through this sort of crisis a hundred times in her life. The first time he had been allowed to watch her work had already been a privilege, and he was strangely giddy that an opportunity had come up again so soon. But he realised why Celine had offered to take him with her—or at least he thought he knew.

She wasn't comfortable with him watching their daughter on his own. Though he understood her hesitancy, what puzzled him was the tension snapping into place between them every time they met. It had happened suddenly at the beginning, with Darius dismissing his own feelings for her—writing them off as an anomaly. He'd thought they would fade away as they interacted with each other, once they understood what kind of relationship they wanted to have now that they were co-parents.

His feelings had not faded, but rather grown with an intensity that made him balk. No, grown wasn't the right word. He recognised these feelings, knew them as he knew the back of his hand—like he knew what bones were in that hand, what their names were. What was blooming inside his chest was the tiny kernel of affection for Celine that had never died, despite his multiple attempts to smother it.

Darius had felt responsible for his mother's wellbeing since he was twelve, when an accident had killed his father, and the bond between them had only deepened over the years. Without his father or any siblings, they'd only had each other.

He now knew that his mother had kept him trapped at her side with the only bond she knew would get him—family. Darius had been raised to believe that his family would be worth any sacrifice, any hardship. It was something he still believed to this day, though the definition of family had changed. Blood relations had little to do with who he now considered his family. Especially when his mother had fabricated the evidence that had kept him away from Celine—making him believe he'd stayed away for her sake. He'd had to choose between one family or the other, his choice having consequences through the years.

No wonder she didn't trust him alone with their child. He still had a lot of work to do to regain the trust that he had broken. And the first thing he needed to do was push those re-emerging feelings back down and never let them see the light of day.

No, it was what came with that attraction, that desire, that he must suppress if he wanted that dynamic to work. Darius had already lost five years of his daughter's life. He wasn't going to miss any more of it just because he couldn't control the fire erupting in his veins every time he came close to his estranged wife. Reconciliation couldn't factor into any of his decisions.

His goal was to get to know his daughter, repair the trust between them enough so Celine would be willing to let Nina out of her sight without worrying too much and, once he had secured his contract with the team, he would be able to finally give her the divorce she wanted. Set her free.

The thought twisted his stomach, and he swallowed the wince that it brought to him. The pangs of jealousy he felt whenever he pictured Celine moving on from him were not only pathetic, they were also inappropriate.

They hadn't been husband and wife for a long time—for as long as they had been married, he realised with profound sadness.

Darius found himself at a crossroads again, knowing he could only choose one side—and it had to be his daughter. If he lost Nina again just because he was chasing some remembered feelings for her mother, he would never forgive himself.

'What's the game plan?' he asked when she hopped out, grabbing the bag of supplies she had tossed into the flat bed of the truck.

'Game plan?' Celine looked at him with a raised eyebrow.

'Sorry, sports metaphor. How are we going to treat the horse?'

She chuckled at that, a sound so lovely and bright that his blood heated, the urge to fold her into his arms and never let her go surfacing with an unexpected ferocity. 'You call a treatment plan a game plan?'

'I work with professional athletes. They appreciate when I speak their language.' He shot her a grin as he added, 'You're just jealous that you don't know how to speak horse.'

'Excuse you, but I am fluent in horse. Clearly you don't remember how I treated Roach's abscess when there were little to no symptoms. How else could I have known that?'

Celine narrowed her eyes at him, then started towards the stables.

As he closed the door with a thud, Juliana's head appeared out of one of the enclosures and she waved them towards her. Darius met Celine's eye and she nodded. Gone was the soft expression their joking had put on her face, replaced with a compassionate determination that was the essence of her professional persona.

'Thank you for coming so fast,' Juliana said as Celine stepped into the enclosure. 'I think the foal is not sitting right in the birth canal.'

Worry laced the farmer's voice, her deep care for her animals tangible. She stepped aside to grant Celine admission, and Darius chose to stay outside and give her enough space to work, ready to help if she needed him.

Celine set the bag down and pulled on a pair of latex gloves that reached all the way up to her shoulders. He watched with intent as she stepped up to the mare and stroked her nose as she whispered words Darius couldn't quite hear from his vantage point.

'We'll get you and your foal sorted, lovely,' he heard Celine say as she walked over to her bag and grabbed her stethoscope, holding it against the horse's abdomen and listening with closed eyes for a few moments.

'The foal is still alive, that's good news. You were right to call me when you did, Jules.' She nodded at the other woman, then joined her at the back of the horse to inspect the progress of the birth.

Darius had to resist the urge to ask about what was happening when Celine's face scrunched into a frown of concentration. As if she heard his silent plea, she said, 'It looks like this is the face of the foal. It's almost in position, but not quite. How long has it been since the waters broke?'

'We're almost at thirty minutes,' Juliana replied, and Celine frowned.

She flicked her wrist around to look at her watch, frowning even deeper. Then she lifted her head, looking straight at him. 'Can you give me an update on time every five minutes? We need to work fast but carefully if we want this foal to be birthed alive.'

Darius stood up straight. He hadn't expected to become a part of the procedure. 'Okay,' he said as he looked at his own wristwatch, the situation strangely familiar to the one with Álvaro earlier this morning.

Celine nodded, a grateful smile on her face. 'Juliana, please get your front-loader in here. I need to give her an epidural so we can lift her legs up without her kicking and then shift the foal.'

The farmer nodded and left the stable to retrieve the machinery Celine had requested.

Celine almost laughed at Darius's shocked expression. Though most of the theory of illness and complications were the same—a human baby couldn't spend prolonged time in the mother's birth canal, same as a foal—how they resolved the problems were much different when dealing with a being that weight half a ton.

'You can't do a C-section? Is that even a thing with horses?' he asked.

'You can perform a C-section on a horse, yes. But we can't do it here. There's another farm twenty minutes from here that has a surgical facility they let me use from time to time, but we wouldn't be able to get there on time.' She looked at the horse, Rosalie, shaking her head. 'This is the best option we have to get mum and foal through this alive.'

The sound of an engine cut through the silence of the stable and Juliana appeared in a green front-loader. She stopped in front of the open enclosure, then lowered the mechanical arm of the vehicle and drove forward. Once positioned right about Rosalie, the arm came down some more before the engine noise died.

Celine stood, everything for the epidural ready in her hands and pockets. 'Grab that rope there and tie it on a loose loop around her waist,' she said to him, her chin pointing towards a coil of thick rope lying on the floor.

As he moved to do that, she grabbed a footstool from the side. Standing on top of it, she looked down at the horse, her fingers gliding over her spinal cord as she counted the vertebrae. When she found the spot she was looking for, she caught Darius's eyes and he held the loose end of the rope.

He immediately looked down at his watch. 'Four minutes and thirty-six seconds.'

'We're good on time, then.' She nodded, then pointed at her bag. 'There are some hair clippers at the bottom, Darius. Please hand them over.'

As her estranged husband dug for the clippers she carried around in her supplies, Celine was overcome with an odd sense of closeness. Though she had only asked him to join her to spare his feelings, she was now glad that she had. Juliana was well versed in being her assistant whenever she was treating larger animals and, even though she had never worked with Darius before, their non-verbal communication was still as good as it had been in their early relationship. Living apart for the last six years had somehow not hurt their connection—it had hurt her heart, though.

When he handed her the clippers she shaved a small patch of hair away, then took the syringe of lidocaine and inserted the needle under the horse's skin to numb the area. Darius's hand was by her side before she could even voice her request, taking the used syringe from her fingers and popping it into a small container inside her bag for biohazardous waste.

'There's a small bottle of saline solution in one of the smaller pouches. Get me that and, while I set the needle, prep another syringe with eight millilitres of lidocaine for the second dose,' she instructed Darius, who handed her the bottle of saline before turning back to the bag to see to her other request.

He might not be a vet but, as a medical professional, he still understood all the jargon she was throwing at him. A fact that she was grateful for as they worked through this high-pressure situation. With a shake of her head, Celine forced herself to focus, unscrewing the bottle and placing a small drop of saline on top of the spinal needle. She palpated the horse's vertebrae again, then inserted the needle in between the space, all the way down through the skin into the spinal cord.

The drop of saline disappeared down the needle, telling her that she had reached where she was supposed to be. When she looked up, Darius was already standing next to her, the lidocaine she had asked for in his hand.

'Thanks,' she said with a smile, then took the syringe and inserted it into the spinal needle, counting beneath her breath to ensure she wasn't pushing the medication in too fast. Once it was administered, Celine removed the syringe and the spinal needle, stepping down from the stool and dragging it back to the side of the enclosure.

'Time?' she asked, and Darius flicked his wrist.

'Eight minutes and two seconds.'

'The epidural takes six minutes to kick in. Once the six minutes are up, we will lift her then settle her back down.' She walked over to Rosalie, palpating her abdomen. 'She is still having strong contractions. I'm positive if we can right the position of her foal, we will be able to birth it. Get ready with the front-loader, Jules,' she said, then positioned herself behind the mare, watching her tail twitch back and forth.

The seconds ticked by slowly and Celine suppressed the nerves rising within her. Though she had been in this situation many times, each foaling was different. There was no one solution. No, each treatment plan was unique to the horse she worked with, and so there was a large margin for error. Confident as Celine was in her abilities, such tricky births could go either way.

An arm wrapped around her shoulders, the strong hand landing on her upper arm as Darius pulled her closer to him in a reassuring gesture. His other hand remained at his side, rising occasionally for him to look at his watch.

He radiated warmth into her body where her side touched his, the knot between her shoulders slowly relaxing as his thumb grazed over her arm in a calm and reassuring rhythm that instantly set her at ease—way more than his touch should. But her nerves were so fried, the day such a whirlwind of different emotions, culminating in the emergency delivery of a foal, that she couldn't spare the mental and emotional energy to contemplate why his body pressing against hers was flooding her with warmth and tranquillity the way little else could do in this situation.

So Celine let herself lean into the touch, cherishing the moment for what it was and resisting attributing any deeper meaning to it.

Darius knew how stressful these treatments could be, was a doctor himself, so he was providing her with support in a difficult professional setting and nothing else. The heat pooling within her stomach was from exertion, not from his scent drifting up her nose and filling her head with old memories of other times they had pressed their bodies against each other.

His hand fell from her arm when the mare's tail went limp, and all three of them sprang into action. Juliana, who was already sitting in the front-loader, looked at her, and Celine nodded, giving her the signal to lift the arm of the machine in a controlled but fast motion, pulling the mare's legs up into the air. A loud whinny echoed through the stables, one that was picked up by several other horses as they whinnied in solidarity with their friend.

Celine pointed towards the mare's head, and Darius moved, laying his hand on her neck and stroking up and down.

'I have her legs secured,' she shouted as she held onto either side of Rosalie. 'Let her down slowly.'

Juliana did so, lowering her down centimetre by centimetre until her hooves were back on the floor. As she did so, Darius moved to untie the rope and drag it out of the way while

Celine inspected the foal's progress. 'It seems to be in the right position now, but she may need some more help,' she said as she moved away from the back and palpated the abdomen again. 'With her next contraction, let's do manual traction to help the foal further along.'

Juliana nodded, then moved to the other side, placing her hand to mirror Celine's.

'Darius, I need you to stand behind Rosalie. Should the foal come fast, you need to ease it onto the floor. There are some disposable aprons and another pair of gloves in my bag.'

Celine thought he was going to balk at the idea of catching the foal but, to her surprise, he simply nodded then put on the apron and gloves before positioning himself behind the horse. Over the last week, she had thought many times that he would shirk away from difficult tasks or conversations, find the easy way out instead. That was what he had done six years ago, so she had no reason to believe this time would be any different. But at every single opportunity Darius had surprised her, standing his ground and facing any difficulties head-on. Had she been misjudging him all this time, letting the hurt he had inflicted on her blind her so much that she couldn't see the change in him?

Was it time to give him another chance?

The sensation of her side pressed against him, his arm around her shoulder as if it belonged there, surfaced in her mind, and she pushed it away as Rosalie's abdomen tightened. 'She is about to contract, Jules,' she said, and the other woman grunted. As they felt the spasms they pushed the foal along to re-enter the birth canal.

'I can see something… Hooves?' Darius didn't sound sure, so Celine walked over to him, letting out a sigh of relief when she saw a pair of hooves and, further down, the small nose of the foal.

'Graças a Deus,' she whispered her thanks, then reached inside to wipe the membrane and other fluids from the foal's mouth to make it easier to breathe. 'With the next contraction, I will pull enough so the head gets out. Once that's done, the hardest part is over and we just need to help Rosalie get over the finish line.'

He nodded, and she raised her eyebrows in question as a grin tugged on his lips. He leaned forward, his mouth close enough that, even in the heat of the stable, she could feel his breath grazing her cheek. 'Thanks for the sports metaphor,' he said, then retreated a step.

The shiver rising through her was the last thing she needed right now. She placed her palm flat on the mare's abdomen again, waiting for signs of the next contraction.

'Here she goes,' she whispered to herself, then removed her hand and reached to grab the already visible hooves to pull in time with the contraction.

Celine grunted as she pressed her feet into the floor, regulating her strength as she helped Rosalie with this tricky birth. Too much force could tear the umbilical opening in the abdominal wall, but too little wouldn't help the foal progress through the birth canal. She just needed to get the head out and the rest would follow.

'There we go,' she huffed, her hands dipping down behind the ears and helping the rest of the head out and into the air.

She looked up, her hand open to request a towel, but, before she could even voice her wish, a soft towel hit her outstretched palm. Her eyes rounded. How could he have known she needed a towel? She was covered in amniotic fluid and bits of the membrane that had surrounded the foal—none of which particularly bothered her since it came with the job. The towel in her bag could have easily been for her, yet he had somehow picked up that she needed it for the foal.

Five more minutes and two more contractions and the foal was born, Darius standing next to her and helping her catch the young horse, placing it on a pile of straw behind its mother.

'Get behind the boundary now, *amor*,' she said, half distracted as she rubbed the towel all over the foal to get the fluids off and encourage breathing. 'Her maternal instincts can kick in just like that, and she'll go from docile to aggressive.'

Darius stared at her for a second, then walked across the enclosure and back behind the wooden half door that kept him separate from the mare while Celine began a thorough check on foal and mare.

Amor. The word had shocked Darius to his core, setting his heart at a pace that it could not sustain as he walked out of the horse box as she'd requested. Celine had seemed distracted, the fifty minutes they'd spent birthing this foal leaving her skin with a sheen of sweat and other stickier things that he for one couldn't wait to wash off in a long and hot shower.

Juliana had hovered around, following the inspection closely, though if Celine looked tired then the farmer had looked downright exhausted as she had swayed on her feet. Celine had noticed it too, for she had dismissed the woman. The two women seemed to share a close rapport that he meant to ask Celine about. Though all the football players on his team were technically his patients, he considered some of them also his friends. Maybe the same could be true for the owners of the livestock that Celine treated.

While all of this had been happening Darius's mind was reeling, the word of affection so casually spoken finding its way into his heart and bringing back the emotions that he had spent so much time locking up. Watching her work had filled him with awe, her compassion and decisive action were traits he'd always admired in her.

Now he sat on the floor outside Rosalie's box, his back leaning against the wood. He looked up as Celine stepped out, closing the door and pulling the gloves and apron off to reveal the clothing beneath free of any stains. She shot him a quick smile, then walked across the stable to where a sink stood tucked away. When she came back a couple of minutes later, her face and hands were wet as she slid down onto the floor next to him. The look she shot him was veiled, not betraying any of the thoughts in her mind.

Was she thinking about what she had said, the way he was? Or didn't she even realise that with one tiny word she had set his mind spiralling, trying to find meaning in something that didn't mean anything?

So he said the first thing that came into his mind. 'I thought you had brought me with you out of pity, but turned out you really needed some extra hands.'

Celine closed her eyes, her head falling back as she took a couple of deep breaths. Without opening them again, she said, 'I can always use extra hands when handling livestock and larger animals, so your help was welcome. But… I *did* invite you to lessen the blow as well.'

That confession didn't surprise him much, as he had sensed it the moment the invitation had left her lips. He wasn't offended by it, but rather intrigued. 'You still care enough about me to spare my feelings.'

A fact she couldn't deny. Why else would she have even hesitated a second to enforce a reasonable boundary around who got to look after her child? Or was there a hidden desire to spend more time with him alone?

The dark blush rising to her cheeks confirmed his suspicion that she herself had realised there was a deeper meaning in why she hadn't simply sent him home when she'd got the emergency call.

'And what about it?' Celine lifted her head

again, her eyes fluttering open to look at him with the same unreadable expression. 'I care about the father of my child, have done so since she was born.'

He held his breath as she spoke, expecting her to throw his abandonment of her in his face—even though he would have been on the next flight back had he known back then that she was pregnant. Hadn't he admitted to enough fault at this point?

Darius would regret leaving for the rest of his life. Because of the five years of his daughter's life that he'd missed, yes. But also because he had left the one woman he had ever loved. Because he had unwittingly let her struggle through years of single motherhood when he could have been there to help.

'I didn't mean it like that,' he said, hoping his appeasing tone would lower her hackles. 'I'm glad I was here to help. Not sure how you would have done it with just Juliana here.'

Celine shrugged, clearly not as concerned as he had been about the help she'd needed. 'Usually, her wife or her older kids will help during foaling season. I've also been able to ask Rafael for assistance.'

'Rafael is Maria's husband? The one who drove Álvaro and Bruna home?'

She nodded, a small smile the only sign of

her warm feelings towards the man, and even though Darius knew it was completely irrational, a pang of jealousy rose in his chest that he willed away with a few breaths.

'Maria and Mirabel used to live with us before she got married to Rafael, so childcare used to be a lot easier. I just had to knock on the door and let her know I was on the way out.'

He searched his memories for the name Mirabel, finally stumbling upon it. 'She's your brother's daughter. Why is she living with Maria?'

Celine huffed at that, a laugh laced with a deep hurt that radiated from her like a sizzling flame, making him turn his head back to her to watch her expression. There was a strange resignation in her eyes, as if she had answered the question he'd asked her too many times.

'Daniel almost brought our family charity to its knees when he fell in love with the wife of our biggest benefactor. They ran away together, we don't even know where.' She paused, voice frosty as she added, 'He didn't care enough to take his daughter with him. Maria took Mirabel in, treats her like her own daughter. So does Rafael. Daniel shouldn't have left, but that little girl got the family she deserves.'

Tension snapped into place between them

as he sensed the hidden meaning behind her words. Was that message aimed at his shortcomings? Darius knew that words alone would not be enough to convince her of his intentions, but he had not relied solely on words. No, he had stuck around, spent a week in Santarém so he could get to know his daughter, tried to become a part of her life.

'I wouldn't have left had I known about Nina,' he said, his voice low as he steeled himself for her rebuttal.

But her smile was soft and sad as she looked at him, a sigh falling from her lips before she said, 'I know you would have stayed. If you had done a worse job of cutting me out of your life, you might have heard about her. I certainly didn't *want* to raise her on my own.'

The gentleness was unexpected, hitting him in a low place and pushing the air out of his lungs. He'd prepared himself for her fury, knew how to withstand it. But this resigned regret was something wholly new to him and he didn't know how to process that.

'Was it hard for you to do it on your own?' It was a question that had been occupying his thoughts for a long time. Though he hadn't meant for her to go it alone, that was still how it had happened.

Celine considered, then gave a small nod.

'Her birth was tough. I had to learn everything on my own. That's actually how I met Juliana. She and her wife were at one of the birthing classes. When they told me they run a farm a few kilometres away from Santarém, I couldn't believe my luck. We became friends and working partners that day.' She paused, the warm feelings for Juliana clearly written in her face. 'The next low point was Nina's first birthday. I was by myself, didn't want Maria to make a big deal out of it because…a first birthday is something for the parents to celebrate. Nina doesn't remember anything about that day. That was a moment for me… For you.'

Darius's throat tightened at the melancholy in her voice. How could he ever give her those moments back? 'I'm sorry, Cee…'

It was Celine's turn to shift her gaze forward to scrutinise the wall in front of them.

He traced the soft shape of her jaw with his eyes, his gaze gliding down to her neck and resisting the urge to bury his face there to drink in more of her scent. God, even after six years, she was still the most stunning woman on the planet. How could he have walked away from her? Looking back at his choices, the sacrifices his mother had demanded in the name of family seemed too much to ask of anyone.

And as if she was picking up traces of his

thoughts, she turned her head towards him again, a plea written in her amber eyes. He knew what she was about to ask even before she said the word.

'Why?'

Darius had known that the small amount of information he'd given her when they'd come to this farm the first time around would not appease her. She needed the whole story—even though there were so many whys to cover. So many things he didn't want to say.

Darius took a deep breath. He'd been steeling himself for this moment and had decided over the last week that if she wanted to know, he would tell her the truth. If it had been just about getting a divorce, he wouldn't have needed to expose himself like that, let her see his failure as a husband. But there was more at stake now. They had a daughter and, because of that, they would be a part of each other's lives for ever.

'When my mother said we had to leave Brazil, she made it sound like this was her choice, and that Brazil had just outlived its usefulness for our family business,' he said, his voice steady even though his heart was pushing against his chest.

'Her cosmetics brand was quite popular when I was a teen. Every girl in my class had a different colour of Delgado lip gloss so we could compare.' Celine chuckled at the memory. 'I was very starstruck to know that you were her son.'

'Her brand's sales had been in steady decline, with fewer and fewer stores picking up new products and shipments—to the point that she announced we were leaving, as there would be more favourable market conditions back in Peru.'

Celine nodded. 'I know this part of the story, Darius. You asked me to marry you so you could stay with me—to be together and make our own family. Only you never came back.'

Darius swallowed, his throat tightening as he considered the next part of the story. 'When we arrived in Peru, I started my application for a spouse visa. I told my mother that I was leaving, and…that was when she told me we'd *fled* Brazil because some shady creditors were after her when she'd defaulted on her business loans.' He paused, the memory of that conversation rising in his mind's eye. 'Along with a terminal diagnosis.'

Celine's eyes widened at that, her lips parting in a sound of surprise. 'Leona died?'

He nodded, the grief in his chest so heavily intertwined with the fury and regret her lies had inflicted on him that he couldn't feel one without the other. 'She had liver cancer, the slow kind that takes years but has a low survival rate. She pressured me into staying, told me I was the only one who could help her fix the business—that I would need to be the one to continue the Delgado legacy.'

He sighed, hardly able to believe how much he had sacrificed for his mother in her dying days, believing that what she'd told him was the truth. 'She said that I couldn't go back to Brazil, that the people she'd borrowed money from would be after me, and that they would be after you too. When she learned I had married you, she seemed genuinely concerned for your safety. So she convinced me to stay, to help her with the business and then find someone to run it since I had my mind set on being a doctor.'

As he spoke, his gaze dropped to the floor, his vision blurry as he struggled to keep his tone even. The words had tumbled out as if he had been desperate to say them after all of these years. Darius wasn't looking for forgiveness, hadn't even planned on telling her as much as he already had. She would think him an idiot to have believed his mother's words so readily.

The rustling of straw drew his gaze, and he looked straight into Celine's eyes, his breath shuddering at the warmth he found there. She had shifted closer to him, her hand on his knee in silent encouragement. He couldn't help but smile, the touch radiating comfort through him.

'She told you I would be in danger if you came back here?' she asked, her voice soft and even.

'Yes. She showed me the communication she'd had with these loan sharks—people she'd turned to after the banks wouldn't give her any more money. There I saw they knew my name, your name and people in our circle, along with threats of harm. I was…shocked to learn that my mother was involved with these people.'

He laid his hand over hers, curling his fingers around it as he continued, finally revealing the truth. 'So I cut off contact, too scared that something might happen to you. But when I started digging into the problems in the business, I encountered…inconsistencies in her story. Things didn't add up, but every time I confronted my mother she would deny it, or change the subject. I could see how hard chemotherapy was hitting her, so how could I push her?'

Darius swallowed, thinking back to how much time he had spent going over the mountain of documents associated with the Delgado brand, and how much money she had sunk into a failing business, not willing to give up. 'Then she died, and I gained access to some documents she had been hiding until the very last day. There were no loan sharks, only legitimate banks and private investors demanding their money back. She had forced us to leave Brazil to escape them, knowing that they couldn't touch her in Peru. All the messages and emails she'd shown me had been fabricated, the people behind them no more than ghosts. I found out I had given up the most precious thing in my life because of my mother's lies…and I couldn't even confront her about it.'

The sound of him swallowing was audible in the silence. Celine still held his hand, her chest rising and falling in an even rhythm as she looked at him, none of her thoughts written on her face. He didn't know if she believed him, wasn't sure he would have believed someone if they had told him that story.

'Why did she lie?' she asked, giving voice to a question he'd spent countless hours contemplating.

'My father was the primary breadwinner. Before his death, making skincare products had been nothing more than a hobby for her. When he passed, she became responsible for both of us. She worked so hard to achieve success, I don't think she could let it go. Not without knowing that someone else would take care of what she'd built over the years.' He paused to sigh. Darius had no way of knowing if his theory was correct. A part of him believed his mother had misled him for her own gain, but another part couldn't see her acting in her self-interest like that. For his own peace of mind he needed to believe that she'd had good reasons, even if he couldn't understand them.

He continued. 'I think her diagnosis scared her, and I was the only person she thought could help her. That doesn't make it right, and I also don't mean that as an excuse. The choices I made were mine, even if based on lies.'

Finally, a frown tugged on her lips as she said, 'You should have told me…'

He huffed a bitter chuckle. 'I know that now. But back then I was too scared they would find you if I gave you any details—didn't know that none of this was real. I was worried that if I told you, you'd try to help.'

It was Celine's turn to chuckle, but there was no trace of bitterness in her voice. 'I probably would.'

Darius found it in himself to laugh, the weight of this secret he'd been carrying around lifted. Regret still burned in his veins whenever he thought of the chances he'd lost because he had been too blind to see. But he knew there was no point in wallowing in what was lost. All that was left to do was to move forward, to be a father to his daughter.

His grip tightened around her hand. 'I'm not asking you to forgive me. But I need you to know that I'm sincere when I say that I want to be a part of Nina's life.' He hesitated as an idea formed in his head. 'The summer holidays start next month, right? Why don't you and Nina visit me in São Paulo? A little family holiday, if you will.'

A part of him thought he was moving too fast, that Celine would push him back. She didn't trust him yet, at least not enough to leave Nina in his care without her supervision. But, to his surprise, she nodded, turning her hand around so she could return his squeeze with one of her own.

'Let's do that. These are the last days of foaling season, so I can take some time off. It'll be good for Nina to see where you live and get comfortable spending time in the big city,' she said, and Darius's heart leapt at that. There was nothing more exciting than the thought of having his daughter visit him.

Maybe one thing was equally exciting, a little voice whispered as his fingers grazed her palm and noticed the tiny shudder running through her body.

* * *

The glint in his eyes was so alluring, the warmth in them inviting her to lose herself by just staring into them for the rest of eternity. Each stroke of his fingers against her palm sent fire through her veins, setting every centimetre of her skin alight until she could no longer suppress the shivers that shuddered through her.

Celine stared down at her hand, willing it to let go of him, but it was no longer hers to command.

She was still reeling from what he had told her, the agony in his voice as he'd told her the truth something she would remember for a long time. He'd left because he'd been led to believe staying would put him in danger—would put *her* in danger. Celine tried to put herself in that situation, tried to understand what her reaction would have been, and with each new scenario that unravelled in her head, she came to the same conclusion.

She would have told him, risks be damned. Maybe that would have been dumb, but Darius had been the love of her life. Her other half. How could she not have trusted him with this information? She could understand his decision—and learning the truth set her heart at ease. But that he hadn't trusted her with this showed their marriage had been doomed to fail from the very beginning.

'I believe you, Darius,' she said, giving him a small smile that threatened to spill over into a larger one when she saw relief wash over his features. 'And I decided to move on from what had happened between us when you first met Nina. I figured we wouldn't be good co-parents if I held so much negativity for you in my heart.'

Her eyes dipped low when he swallowed, watching his throat bob, and on the way back up her eyes stopped on his lips, remaining there. The heat already circulating through her body gathered into a tight cluster in the pit of her stomach that gradually dropped lower, setting her core on fire and summoning the ghost of pleasure she'd found lying beneath those skilful lips.

'You are as kind as I remember, Cee,' he said, then lifted both of their hands to the lips she had just been fantasising about and blew a soft kiss onto her skin. 'I will not let this second chance go to waste.'

Her hand lingered against his lips, the feel of them so hauntingly familiar on her skin, the pleasure they could give one she had gone without for years—all her energy going into raising her daughter. She hadn't realised how much she had missed small affections like this. How big a gap Darius had truly left in her life. Not only as the father of her child and as her husband, but…as a friend. As a lover.

A slight tremble shook her hand as she extended her fingers towards him. He inhaled a sharp breath when her fingertips brushed over his lips, then wound their way over his jawline to his cheekbone, tracing the powerful line. Her body was no longer hers to control, each action coming from a place of need that she had ignored over the years—the person embodying all of that desire absent from her life.

But now he was right here, and the feelings she had been pushing away with such force over the last week burst back to life at that tiny brush of his lips against her flesh. A touch she wanted more of—all over her body.

Celine leaned forward, her face now close enough for their noses to touch. 'Maybe we can be friends again,' she whispered, shuddering as his breath swept across her heated cheeks.

'I would like that,' he replied, voice thick with the same desire and anticipation that had been rising in her ever since he'd stepped back into her life.

'But we need to stop with this,' she said, making no attempt at stopping at all.

'Yes, that would be wise.' In contrast with

his words, his hands moved up to her face, cupping each side and then pulling her down, closing the remaining space between them.

The kiss was unexpected, its power shaking her to her core. Her hands went up to his chest, winding themselves into the fabric of his shirt and clinging onto him as if to ground her in this moment. A familiar taste filled her mouth as his tongue swept over her lips, then entered her with a soft groan that vibrated through her skin.

Need she had been suppressing broke free like floodwater from a dam, flooding her system and wiping away the doubts and worries that surrounded her relationship with Darius. The only thing she could focus on was the heat, the feeling of profound familiarity as his hands brushed down her sides, gripping her and making her forget where she was and who she was with—the clarity of knowing what to expect from this kiss chasing away any doubts.

Celine shuddered when his arms wrapped around her, one hand pressed against the small of her back, the other one on her chest and pushing her down until she lay on the floor—Darius's familiar weight between her legs. His hip pushed against hers and she writhed against his hardness.

With his scent filling her nose and his lips

working their way down her neck, she couldn't remember the reasons she'd wanted to keep him at arm's length, thought herself silly to deny herself the pleasure of this man when he knew exactly how to touch her—how to drive her wild.

The loud creak of iron hinges swinging open ripped through the luscious cloud Darius had woven around her, and she straightened herself with a start. The sudden return to reality doused her like a bucket of ice water, and she pushed her husband off her.

Her head whipped around to see Juliana walking towards them. By the time the farmer arrived in front of Rosalie's enclosure, she and Darius had climbed to their feet and righted any items of clothing that had shifted.

Celine's pulse hammered in her throat as she looked at Juliana, the other woman's smirk telling her she knew exactly what had been going on.

'You're back early,' Celine said, though she didn't know how much time had passed. Once the mare had birthed the placenta and she had given them another check-up, she had retreated from the box. She had told Juliana to come back in three hours as that would be enough time to ensure the placenta had been delivered and observe any side-effects from the difficult birth.

'It's been almost four hours,' Juliana said, and from the corner of her eye she saw Darius look at his wristwatch and heard him utter a low curse in Spanish.

'Well…' Celine hesitated, searching for the right words. Her brain was scrambled with all that had happened in the last few hours, and it took her far too long to remember the reason she had been lying on the floor of her client's stable to begin with.

'Rosalie is all good. She birthed the placenta. The foal is a bit rattled but breathing and taking milk. The worst is behind us. I'll come back in a couple of days to check on them.' She looked at Juliana, a silent plea in her eyes to not say anything else, and, to her eternal relief, she did just that, giving her only a nod.

Celine grabbed her pack off the floor, hoisting it onto her shoulder, then dared a quick glance at Darius. His expression was unreadable, the flames she had seen in his eyes gone and nothing but some redness around his mouth betraying what had just gone on between them.

CHAPTER SEVEN

THE NERVES THAT had been fluttering in his stomach for the last couple of hours flared into a raging fire as the status of the flight from Manaus changed to 'Arrived'.

With the Copa América having played its final game last week, his team had come back to São Paulo to get ready for the next season of the Brasileirão—the most prestigious national league of Brazil. Though there wouldn't be any matches for another three weeks, the players were back on their usual training schedule so they would be ready for the first rounds. Having spent so much time playing for the national team, a few players needed extra care to avoid injury, so Darius had been watching them train every day.

But more than once these past two weeks, Celine had sneaked into his mind, the memory of their kiss in the stables popping up out of nowhere and robbing him of his composure.

The kiss had been the final concession he'd made, the last battle he'd lost against the resurgence of his feelings for Celine—his wife.

Though he knew now that this had been one of the dumber mistakes he had made in recent weeks. Darius didn't know what it was about that night that had prompted him to share his story with her, but he had told her—and she had understood. Forgave him, even. It was that last part that made the thought of reconciliation so tangible, the way forward seemingly less daunting. The kiss had only helped to illuminate the path towards a happy ending for their marriage. An ending where they would become the family both of them had always dreamed of. All the elements were already there, they had to simply reach out and grab it.

Yet every time that thought arose, Darius batted it away, pushing it down and into obscurity, only for it to bounce back up into his consciousness. There was no way towards reconciliation, no matter what his brain conjured up in idle moments. His priority was his daughter and forming that relationship, not running after the wife he had been tricked into forsaking.

What had happened at Juliana's farm was a lapse of judgement and could never happen again—even though he yearned to have another taste of her, not having known that was the last time they would kiss. Just like he hadn't known six years ago... Would he ever have enough of Celine?

The way his pulse sped up when he saw her step through the doors told him the answer was probably no.

Celine and Nina were scanning the crowd, looking for him, and when their eyes locked on him both their faces lit up with smiles that kicked his heart into overdrive. Instead of lusting after the woman he couldn't have, he should be thankful that a mere visit caused such a joyful reaction in them.

Nina broke into a sprint as she saw him, leaving her mother behind as her tiny legs carried her over to him. Darius crouched down, extending his arms to sweep her into a hug that immediately set him at ease, dousing any nerves that were bubbling in the pit of his stomach.

This was why he had to keep his distance. Anything that threatened the relationship he was building with Nina was off-limits—that included his own feelings for her mother. He would not risk any more. What if they reconciled, and it didn't work out? It would devastate Nina. Their relationship had only just formed, his young daughter becoming more comfortable with him each time they saw each other.

'Darius!' she yelped with a giggle as he picked her up off the floor, heaving her onto his hip, and praying his face didn't show the stab of disappointment on hearing his name. He had no right to demand to be called Pai—Dad. Yet a part of him hoped she would say it every time they spoke.

'Hola, mi princesa preciosa. Cómo estás?' he said, earning himself a puzzled look from his daughter.

'Que?' she asked, though her attention was immediately drawn to the balloon he was holding by a string. 'Is that for me?'

Before he could answer, Celine stepped up to them, dragging a suitcase behind her. 'He asked you how you are, *filha.*'

'Oh.' Nina's lips rounded as the sound escaped her mouth, her eyes still snagging on the balloon. Whatever her mother had said had gone in one ear and out the other.

Darius laughed at that, then handed his daughter the string before he set her down on the floor. Then he turned to Celine, his hand going up to her arm and greeting her with a kiss on her cheek. Only when his lips brushed her skin did he realise that the way to greet someone that was ingrained in South

American culture maybe hadn't been the best move with all the unresolved feelings floating around between them.

He sensed the rippling of her muscles under his fingertips, but she didn't reveal anything and just smiled at him.

'Let me get that for you,' he said, reaching for her suitcase to distract himself from the heat rising in his chest—heat he had banished to the far corners of his being, which had no business re-emerging at this moment.

He led them through the airport to the car park, loading everyone into the car and driving them to his apartment in the heart of São Paulo. Both Nina and Celine stared wide-eyed as they drove through the city, pointing at the high-rise buildings reaching into the sky—including the one Darius lived in.

By the time he had ushered them into his apartment and given them the tour of his two-bedroom penthouse, Nina had made herself comfortable on his couch and promptly fell asleep on his lap. As he stroked her soft hair and looked down at her tranquil face, his heart was about ready to burst with the unconditional love that had grown tenfold ever since he'd heard about his daughter.

A soft chuckle from Celine tore him out of his observation, and he raised his eyes to meet hers. 'She was up at five packing her little backpack for her trip to see you,' she said, melting his heart even further.

'She was excited to see me?' His voice was low, almost not daring to ask that question. Ever since he had become a part of Nina's life he had braced himself for the inevitable rejection, that Nina would decide that his effort was too late.

His thoughts must have shown on his face, for Celine scooted closer on the couch, laying her hand over the one that had been stroking Nina's hair. 'Relax, Darius. She's comfortable with the idea of her father being in her life.'

He mustered a half smile at her words, the worry still eating at his insides. Everything between them was so fresh, so…fragile. Just one more reason to keep his and Celine's relationship on a strictly co-parenting level.

'I didn't know I could love someone so much,' he said, his voice quiet with wonder and reverence.

Celine nodded, understanding exactly what he meant. 'I know. I grew attached to her as she was growing inside me. But nothing compares to that moment when they put her in my arms for the first time.'

'Should I put her in bed?'

She looked at the clock hanging from his wall. 'What's the plan for today?'

'I thought we could go to Paulista and have a walk there since it's Sunday. Have lunch at the Japan House and check out the street stalls.'

'Um… You'll have to repeat that because I'm not sure what you just said.' Celine looked at him with a furrowed brow, her head slightly tilted.

'You've never been to São Paulo?' he asked and chuckled as she shook her head. 'Paulista is the main shopping street and it's usually busy with traffic—except for Sundays. Every Sunday, the city shuts down traffic to the street and it turns into a large pedestrian area with food stalls, street music and other smaller attractions.'

'Oh…that sounds quite nice. I think she'll enjoy that.' Celine glanced at the clock again. 'We'll let her sleep for an hour. She was up much earlier than she usually is.'

Darius nodded, then scooped his sleeping daughter into his arms and walked to the bed he had put together for her. Tucking her in, he stooped to kiss her on the forehead, then left the room and pulled the door closed behind him—only to find the couch where he had left Celine empty.

He turned around, and then laughed when

she walked back towards him with two cups in her hand. 'Maybe you should take a nap too, if you were up so early,' he said as he took the cup of coffee from her, settling back down on the couch.

Celine shrugged one shoulder, then closed her eyes and savoured the mouthful of coffee with a soft moan that sent his heated blood in entirely the wrong direction. 'Coffee is better. I don't think I could sleep later if I take a nap now.'

'I'm sure we'll find something fun to do once Nina is in bed for the night.' The words flew out of his mouth before he could reconsider them, going against everything he had told himself in the weeks leading up to their visit.

Celine's eyes rounded, clearly not oblivious to the sexually charged subtext in his words. Silence spread between them, the tension snapping into place so tight he felt a tiny breeze could crack it.

Though two weeks had passed, they hadn't spoken about *the kiss*. Darius had left early the next day, needing to get back to São Paulo as training sessions had started again, and Celine hadn't brought it up either. All their texting up to this point had been about the logistics of getting here.

He watched the rise and fall of her chest as she took some breaths, tension mingling with the hunger slumbering inside of him, making him want to reach out and grab the release he saw right in front of him.

Celine stared at Darius, her heart beating in her chest in an erratic dance as she waited for him to say something—though what exactly she wanted him to say, she wasn't sure. Wasn't quite certain what to say in this situation either. That their kiss had haunted her ever since it happened? That the phantom of his lips sneaked onto hers every time she had an unguarded moment, yearning for them to find an excuse to be together again? No, late night impromptu kisses were off the menu. Because, even though Nina's liking of Darius was almost infectious, Celine couldn't forget what had happened between them. He'd explained the situation to her, and she understood and had meant it when she'd said she was ready to move on.

But when she had decided to move on, she hadn't meant to fall straight back into the patterns of their old relationship. Her goal was still to get a divorce, so she could finally find her missing piece. Even though her heart was currently trying to convince her that Darius might just be that person she was looking for, it was not possible.

Even if she could ever overcome the wounds his abandonment had caused her, sitting in his apartment in São Paulo, she realised their lives weren't compatible any more. She needed to be in Santarém to help her sister with the charity while Darius had built his career here.

The kiss had been a mistake. A delicious, mind-blowing mistake which had been on her mind ever since it had happened—and filling her with feelings she had believed long forgotten.

Celine bit back a sigh as she realised they would have to get it over with right now, while Nina was still sleeping.

'You want to talk about it?' she forced herself to say, reading the message in his eyes.

His eyes narrowed on her. 'Do you?'

She couldn't stop the laugh rising in her throat. 'No…but I think this week will be awkward if we don't.'

Darius huffed a laugh at that, some of the tension between them softening at the sound, and Celine found herself smiling as well— remembering how much she had loved his laugh.

'Life has been a lot less…fun without you.' The words had formed in her head as she relished his laugh, its timbre drawing out all the cherished memories of what they had shared in their relationship, with Darius clowning around so much that she couldn't even remember how she used to have fun without him.

His expression softened, warmth warring with an ancient pain that she knew all too well.

'I mean, it's not like I haven't enjoyed life, don't get me wrong. My life has been great,' she quickly added, cringing at how defensive the words had come out.

'Tell me more about it,' he said, his coffee mug dangling from his hand in a gesture so casual that it clashed with the intensity in his gaze. Was he trying to seem nonchalant?

Celine paused, then asked, 'Tell you about what?'

'The last few years. Tell me what I missed.'

'What an…incredibly broad question.' She smirked at him but didn't get the laugh she had been aiming for to cut the tension. No, Darius levelled a smouldering look at her, his dark eyes ablaze with a fire of unknown origin that brought heat to her own cheeks.

A smile appeared on his lips. 'Humour me.'

'Well…' She paused, casting her mind back. 'When I announced I was going back to live in Santarém with my sister, it was an enormous shock to my parents, Maria and the faculty, who thought I was going to stay there to work at the institute for veterinary medicine in Manaus. I didn't tell my sister I was pregnant until I'd been back at home for a few weeks.'

Celine had known that Maria would return and take over the charity from their parents so they could finally ease into their long-awaited retirement in Switzerland.

'And then life in Santarém was much how I remembered it growing up. It was good for Nina to have her aunt and uncle around to give her the attention she needed. And once her cousin Mirabel came to live with us, the two developed an unlikely friendship.' Celine laughed. 'Our working theory is that Nina simply has an old soul.'

Darius laughed, the sound passing through her with a soft shudder that raised the hairs along her arms. 'I can see that, though my experience with five-year-old children is very limited.'

'With Maria's own child in the mix, it'll be interesting to see how she acts as an older cousin.' Nina had already shown great care and gentleness with her newborn cousin Sam, doting on her whenever they went over to Maria's place to visit.

'How well do you get along with your brother-in-law?' He smiled when Celine shrugged her shoulders.

'We hired Rafael when we opened the vet clinic to help cover the costs of the charity after losing our biggest donor to my brother's foolishness. Turns out, Rafael's family is semi-famous, making him the heir to a small fortune.' She paused, considering how much of Maria's story she wanted to tell. 'He grew very attached to Santarém, offered to help and, in the process, they fell in love.'

She looked down into her mug, the light brown liquid making small waves as she swirled it around. 'His arrival made me even more obsolete. Before that, I already didn't have much to do with the charity, other than helping Maria whenever she needed a second opinion. But I've been more of an advisor than a vet to our…her charity. When Rafael started, his interest in furthering the cause became apparent in an instant, so now what small role I had in my family legacy is now gone too.'

Celine's own words hit her with an unexpected ferocity. She blinked several times as emotions she hadn't realised she'd been carrying around welled up. She had always known that she and Maria hadn't been equals in their charity, but Rafael's presence showed her just how much she had detached herself from it.

Darius sensed the thoughts rising in her head, for he put his own mug down on the coffee table and closed some of the distance between them by scooting closer. He didn't touch her, yet his presence was enough to summon warmth to ease away the darkening clouds gathering inside of her.

'Do you regret not playing a larger part in your family charity?' he asked, voicing the nebulous question that had been dancing along the edges of her mind for quite some time, but Celine had been too scared to ever acknowledge it.

Discomfort clawed at her, and she closed her eyes, the breath she took filled with the scent of pine and spice, bringing memories of a simpler time, when they had both been happy with each other.

'No, I don't,' she finally said, her voice barely above a whisper. 'If you had stayed, I think our lives would not have taken us back to Santarém, and that wouldn't have been the worst thing.'

She didn't mean it as an accusation, yet hurt flashed in his eyes at the mention of the life they'd never got the chance to live. It was a thought they both needed to get comfortable with. It was easy to get wrapped up in the disappointments of their past, dream of the what-ifs and how they would have grown closer as a family. But what they needed to think about was the present, and what their relationship needed to be if they wanted to be the best co-parents they could be.

To do that, Darius needed to stop looking at her with those blazing brown eyes, because every time she gazed into them she got lost. But instead of pushing away and extracting herself from his aura, Celine leaned in as she asked, 'If you could go back and make a different choice, would you?'

'Yes.' That was all he said. *Yes.* No elaboration, no recapping of the past mistakes, no additional context to add to that word. Because he didn't need to. The gravel in his voice was all the context she needed to understand the deep regret that accompanied the decision he'd made all those years ago.

Celine held her breath when he reached out, taking hold of her hand and intertwining their fingers. 'I know there's no way back, and I'm not suggesting we should pick things up where we left them. We have a child now, and whatever she needs must come first.' He placed her hand on his chest, covering it with his own, and his heartbeat pulsing beneath her palm sent a shiver down her spine. 'It wasn't my plan to kiss you. I don't know if these feelings are old or new, but the moment got away with me.'

Was this moment getting away with them too? Celine took in a shaky breath, wanting to snatch her hand back, but his warmth radiated through her skin, filling her with a tingling sensation that she hadn't felt in six years. It was the feeling that she wanted to find, the emotion Maria and Rafael got to experience every day—but *not* with Darius. It *couldn't* be him, because how was she ever to trust him again?

'The adrenaline was pumping pretty hard through our veins, so I think we can forgive ourselves for that slip-up,' she said, though the lack of conviction was clear in her voice. She knew intellectually that it had been a mistake, but her heart was saying something else.

Darius's hand dropped from hers, but Celine kept hers pressed against his chest where he had placed it, his strong heartbeat filling her brain with a luscious fog that she was not ready to let go of just yet. His breathing was steady but his eyes darkened as they locked onto hers. A hungry spark flashed in them that turned her core into molten lava.

Then he lifted his hand and slipped it over her neck, cradling the back of it. 'I don't think I ever got over you, Cee,' he said, his voice low with the same desire she'd heard in it two weeks ago.

Everything inside of her wanted to give in, to lose herself in this sensation and to forget her doubts, forget about how he fitted into her life. She swallowed the lump in her throat, her voice breathy as she said, 'Me neither.'

'I tried to move on—tried to find a way forward. But no one has ever caught my attention the way you have.' His thumb grazed over her earlobe, leaving sparks in its wake and filling her head with fantasies of his lips on hers, her neck, her thighs…

'We need some closure,' she replied, grabbing at that word that coalesced in her mind. Because it was not rekindling but closure that was happening between them. Their relationship had ended so abruptly. Of course there were some unresolved feelings.

Darius's thumb slowed at that. 'Closure?'

'We both know there is no path forward for our marriage, Darius. So we need to…have it out and find some closure.'

He stilled, his hand on her neck still sending ripples of desire through her that she tried to douse with logic. The flames in his gaze were banked, the emptiness that filled his eyes so stark that she regretted saying those words. Her hands shot up to his face to cup it, bringing him closer to her as her mind blanked—her only concern to wipe the hurt from his expression as she pulled him into her arms.

Darius stiffened then relaxed against her, his lips replacing his hand on her neck. Goosebumps prickled along her arms and legs as his breath swept over her skin.

'I don't think this is how I will get closure,' he mumbled, his lips brushing over her neck with every word and sending heat lancing through her body.

The world around her faded away, narrowing down to that spot where his lips pressed against her flesh. No other sound or scent or sensation could penetrate that hyper focus, leaving her shivering with need for Darius.

'Darius…' she huffed out as his hands wrapped around her waist, squeezing tight before finding their way upwards—exploring. His name was a plea on her lips and he growled near her ear, his own desire for her taking form.

Then his hands stilled, his muscles tensing underneath her hands as they roamed up his back. She lifted her head to look at him.

Before she could say anything, Darius leaned back, his body no longer in her space, as he said, '*Hola, bella durmiente*. Did you have a nice nap?'

CHAPTER EIGHT

NINA HAD INTERRUPTED them at the wrong time—or was it actually the perfect time? Darius wasn't sure, but he didn't have the mental space to consider what had gone on between him and Celine when their daughter had stepped into the living room. From the look on his wife's face as he had backed off, he could tell that the thought of Nina walking in on this situation had horrified her.

Was Celine right about gaining closure? His mind told him yes, that he was looking exactly for a way to finally move on from her. But that thought didn't reach his heart, which yearned to pull her into his arms and never let her go again. Did it even matter what he wanted? Clearly Celine was ready to put the final notice on their marriage, as she had presented him with divorce papers and spoke of closure. Then why did she keep reaching for him?

After their unceremonious interruption Celine had whisked Nina away to get ready, and they'd spent the rest of the afternoon walking down Paulista Avenue, stopping at various shops and musicians and for one unbelievably delicious ice cream. He'd watched Celine as much as his daughter, enjoying the wonder and excitement in their eyes whenever they spotted something.

By the time they had eaten and were ready to go home, Nina had been so exhausted that Darius had carried her on his back. Now they were back at his place, Nina standing on her feet with her eyes half closed, and Celine looking fairly similar, though he knew from her expression that she tried her best not to show it.

'How about you two get comfortable in your room? We have a whole week's worth of fun activities stacked up, so no need to push so hard,' he said, crouching down in front of his daughter to give her a hug and a kiss on the forehead as the little girl leaned against her mother's legs for support.

He looked up, meeting Celine's equally tired eyes. 'Do you need any help?' he asked, looking back at Nina.

Celine shook her head, then put her hand between their daughter's shoulder blades and pushed her towards the open door of their room. 'Say goodnight to your father, *filha*,' she said as they crossed the threshold.

Nina turned around, giving him a small wave as she said, *'Buenas noches.'*

Darius's eyes widened at her use of Spanish, his native tongue, and kept frozen in place as he stared at the closed door. He'd occasionally sprinkled some Spanish into their conversation, pointing at different things and saying the right words. Not to teach her his language, but to evoke the idea that there was more to her than what she had learned so far. Though Brazil had become his chosen home, and he spoke Portuguese like a native, he was still a Peruvian man, making his daughter part Peruvian.

Maybe further down the line he could help her learn Spanish. The idea warmed him, as did any that involved a future where he was more involved with Nina…and with Celine.

He gave weight to the thought, his mind turning back to the moment they had shared earlier today. He'd spent the time they were apart steeling his resolve, telling himself that there was no path back to where they had been. But the path he was looking onto right now was not the old one that they had walked together before. No, what unfolded in his mind's eye was something completely new, a world full of possibilities that he wanted to reach out and grab with both hands. A reality where they had both learned what they wanted in life, had grown into the people they needed to be, and had then found their way back to each other.

A picture so sublime, so full of love, that Darius immediately pushed it away.

No, he *could not* fall for his wife again. Though he knew his heart, knew that he would never make the same mistakes again, he didn't want to risk anything that could jeopardise his relationship with his daughter. How could they even be together when their lives had grown in such different directions?

Darius let himself fall onto the couch, unbuttoning his shirt and exposing his chest to the chill air in his apartment. His mind was too busy for him to even contemplate sleep, so he lay there in silence instead, his eyes roaming over the dark ceiling as if it had the answer to his problems written on it.

Celine opened her eyes with a frustrated sigh, her hand groping for her phone on the nightstand. She turned on the screen, sighing again when she looked at the time. She'd spent two and a half hours trying to fall asleep, with no success at all. Her thoughts were too loud, her heart racing whenever she thought of how they had spent the day together.

She had rarely seen Nina happier than she'd been today. Having grown up in Santarém with the same people surrounding her every day of every year, her daughter had been excited to explore the city, pointing her finger at every new and exciting thing, asking a million questions as the day went along. Questions that Darius had been more than happy to answer.

Watching them interact, seeing Nina cling to Darius's side at every opportunity, twisted her heart the way nothing else had in the last few weeks. Somehow they had become the family Celine had already dreamed they would be, yet something was missing...something crucial that she needed to complete the picture. That special person in her life to complete her.

The person she'd thought Darius would be when they had met all those years ago.

Quietly, so as not to wake Nina, Celine climbed out of bed and walked towards the door, opening it slowly and closing it behind her with just as much caution. She had to blink a few times to adjust to the light in the living room, the lights of the city filtering in through the large windows. Looking up, the sky was black, the stars she was used to seeing in her remote village wiped away by the brightness of the city itself, millions of people going about their lives.

The day had shown her the appeal of the city life, everything one could ever want at arm's reach, and she'd enjoyed the fantasy of building her own life here. Closer to Darius.

A shiver shuddered down her spine, and she turned away from the window—and stared right into Darius's eyes. He was sitting on the couch, the shirt he'd worn earlier hanging from his shoulders. Her eyes glided downwards, drinking in his exposed chest and abdomen, her fingers prickling at the thought of exploring every plane, ripple and muscle in painstaking detail.

'You're up late,' he said as he straightened himself, giving her an even better view of his body. Her mouth went dry at the sight of it, wetness pooling in other parts of her body.

'Couldn't sleep,' she replied, her breath hitching when he got up in a smooth motion, reminiscent of the wild cats they sometimes treated in the clinic. Watching them stalk up and down their enclosure was a terrifying and impressive sight.

Just like Darius as he walked up to her. Her skin tingled as his eyes swept over her.

'What's keeping you up?' he asked as he approached, her eyes dragging down his body the same way he had checked her out just a moment ago and liking what she saw. *Really* liking what she saw.

His unbuttoned shirt fully exposed his upper body, muscles rippling as he walked, but her gaze dipped further down—following the dark trail of hair as it vanished in his waistband.

He stopped his prowl as he came to a stop in front of her, forcing her to lift her chin to look at him. His eyes were dark, smouldering with a fire that she had seen earlier today— when she had told them they needed distance. Closure. This was the exact opposite of that, yet Celine couldn't fight the attraction. Didn't want to fight it either.

'You,' she breathed, knowing she shouldn't say that, for it stoked the flames in his eyes even higher.

His hand reached out to her, his knuckles brushing over her bare shoulder and down her front, where her peaked nipples were already straining against the silken fabric of her night-dress. She inhaled sharply when he swept over the hardened peaks, his touch no more than a whisper, yet the sensation exploded through her.

'That's funny,' he said, his head coming down towards hers until his lips were right next to her ear. 'You were keeping me up too.'

'Oh, yeah?' Her hands, no longer under the

control of her mind, slid up to his chest, feeling the strong muscles flex underneath her fingertips. Pushing further up, she caught the edges of his shirt and flicked the fabric off his shoulders and down his arms before linking her fingers behind his neck.

Darius chuckled, slipping his hands out of the cuffs. The shirt fell onto the floor and, not even a heartbeat later, his hands were back on her. One pressed against the small of her back, eliminating any space between them. The other one cradled the back of her head, pulling her face towards his.

His lips brushed over hers in a gentle kiss that was enough to send a flood of heat through her core, shivers clawing down her back. She dug her fingers into his shoulders, a low moan leaving her lips when he pulled away ever so slightly.

'I cannot resist you, Celine,' he whispered against her lips, his breath as heavy as hers, each inhale an almost insurmountable feat while their mouths were apart. 'I tried for weeks to forget what you mean to me. Ignore the pull I sense whenever I see you. But I cannot.'

'Darius…' Her eyes fluttered shut when he kissed her again, the gentleness gone and replaced by an urgency that spoke of the restraints he had put himself under—restraints she, too, had practised whenever they had been near each other.

His tongue darted over her lips, then dipped into her mouth as they deepened the kiss, his scent and touch and heat an explosive concoction that robbed her of any clear thought. All she could focus on was the ache building in her core, the flames lapping at her thighs, lancing through her body and driving her desire for him higher and higher.

'Say yes, *amor*,' he said, leaving her mouth to nibble at her earlobe before trailing further down her neck. 'Say yes to me, to us. If the last weeks have shown me anything, it's that you and I belong together.'

Her breath left in a shudder, the onslaught of sensation too much for her to think straight. She should say no. Their relationship was not one to be rekindled. Her heart had barely healed, the shock of seeing him so unexpectedly ripping all of her wounds open again.

Yet he had owned his mistake from the very start, explained his side. She understood why he had left, even though she still disagreed with the way he had handled everything. Would she have done anything different if she'd believed him in danger?

Celine wasn't certain. Six years ago, she

would have done just about anything to keep him safe—including getting married to him so he could stay in Brazil. But she couldn't say yes, not to a future with him still as her husband. The trust in him was too far gone.

'Say yes, Celine. I promise you, I will never hurt you again.' He slid his mouth over hers again, brushing her lips in a gentle kiss that exploded tiny fireworks in her stomach that roared into a fire when his hand slipped under the seam of her nightdress, his nails grazing over her thighs.

Her head fell backwards when his lips brushed over the hollow of her throat, his mouth leaving a burning trail of kisses down to the centre of her breasts while his fingers on her thigh were drawing lazy circles on their way inward.

Her own hands began to wander, roaming over his back in a desperate search for purchase as waves of anticipation and need crashed through her, turning everything inside of her upside down. His scent was so familiar, the brushes of his fingers something she had been yearning for ever since he had left—unable to find anyone like him again.

Celine shuddered when his fingers brushed against the gusset of her underwear, and that was when she cracked wide open, the walls she had built tumbling down as the desire to be with this man overwhelmed her, leaving no room for logic or argument. There was just the passion that was passing between them with every swapped breath.

'Yes,' she breathed, the word hanging in the air.

Darius's hands stilled, his lips stopping their march down her body to come back to her face. His dark gaze bored into hers, then his lips parted in a smile so stunning and genuine that it robbed Celine of her remaining breath. It was just as well, because that meant the yelp she let out was a quiet one as he hoisted her upwards.

She wrapped her legs around his waist to keep her balance as he braced his hands on her butt and walked her towards his bedroom.

Yes. A thrill of triumph had raced through his body at that one syllable that made the hidden desire in his heart he had been denying for the last few weeks an actual reality.

Darius had watched her as she'd stepped out of the room, hard an instant later as his eyes were drawn downwards where the diaphanous fabric swished against the peaks of her breasts. Those feelings came over him unbidden, his control over them wearing thin, and he had feared that the moment would come soon when he wouldn't be able to help himself.

It would have been so easy to forget about it if she hadn't kissed him too. Or kissed him back today. Or if she had simply said no, he could have turned his back and walked away. But now Darius realised he was in way too deep and there was no way out. He *wanted* to be with his wife. Not just in bed, not just this one night or this week they spent together. He wanted her back for good.

For the first time in years his heart felt light, and he could breathe easy again. All thanks to this woman who had her legs wrapped around his waist, her wetness pronounced enough that he could feel it through the barrier of fabric on his skin. The sensation only tightened his erection, and he lengthened his stride, kicking the door shut behind him as they stepped over the threshold.

He dropped her onto the bed and watched from above as she stretched out on his sheets, drinking her in. 'You are stunning,' he whispered, his words prompting her to sit up so her legs were hanging off the bed.

His hand came up to her shoulder, intending to push her back down, but her fingers wrapped around his wrist to stop him. Her eyes were filled with unbridled desire that was reflected in his own. 'Stay right there,' she said, her voice low and full of promises that made him ache.

Then she released his wrist and placed her hands on his abdomen, wandering up towards his chest and caressing the skin there before coming back down, drawing circles as she went and leaving nothing but fire in her wake. He groaned in anticipation as her fingers slipped beneath his waistband, pulling at the fabric without releasing him. His eyes fluttered closed when her breath grazed over his skin and, a moment later, he shuddered when she pressed her lips just below his navel.

Then one of her hands moved to the front of his trousers and, with a flick of her fingers, his button popped open. A sigh fell from his lips as she pulled his trousers down, the discomfort from his trapped manhood subsiding and replaced with a sensation that bordered on discomfort in the most sensual of senses as Celine palmed his length through the fabric of his underwear.

'Celine...' Her name was a plea on his lips, though the edge in his voice left her undeterred from her path.

His hands came to rest on her shoulders, his fingers digging into her flesh as she pulled the remaining layer of fabric that lay between them away. He shuddered as she wrapped her fist around him and pumped in long slow movements, each one a delicious agony he hadn't felt in a long time.

This was almost too much, his muscles so tight under her touch that Darius thought he would explode if he didn't find release soon. That he would be so lucky to get a second chance, to have the opportunity to redeem himself—he hadn't dared to hope ever since he'd stepped back into her life.

And Celine had found it in her heart to see his sincerity for what it was as he'd finally shared the whole story of his disappearance. They would become the family they had always dreamed of.

Then her lips closed around him and his mind went blank, the leash on his passion broken by her touch.

Celine closed her eyes as she took him in her mouth, writhing at the groan that dropped from his lips. His hands, clinging to her shoulders not even a moment ago, roamed down her back, and he balled his fists into the fabric of her nightdress. He drew a muffled chuckle from her as he yanked on it, forcing her face away from him as he pulled it over her head.

When she tried to capture him again, he

stepped backwards and then knelt on the floor. She looked down, and the intent and passion in his eyes caught her breath in her throat. Heat spread in a star shape through her body, rising to her cheeks in a faint blush and settling in her core that contracted in anticipation.

Darius grinned, a look she knew all too well. 'My turn now,' he said, voice filled with gravel that worsened the ache inside. All she could think about was to have him inside of her.

The fabric of her underwear grazed her thighs as he pulled it down, his breath cool on her heated skin as he put both of her legs over his shoulders. But then he took his time, kissing the inside of one knee and trailing his lips and tongue up before repeating the process on the other side. All the while Celine bucked her hips, her body having its own mind that she couldn't override.

All she wanted was his tongue right there where she had been aching for him for weeks.

'You evil, evil man,' she breathed out between clenched teeth as he kissed the apex of her thigh, just above the place she *really* wanted him to kiss.

The breath of his laugh skittered over her skin, raising goosebumps all over her flesh, and he stroked over her thigh, savouring the feel of it.

'Be patient, *amor*,' he whispered, his hand wandering further up to caress her stomach. 'We have the rest of our lives ahead of us.'

Did they, though? That thought managed to push through the fog of lust his touch had elicited in her, drawing her attention to a place she didn't want to be in right now. She hadn't said yes to for ever, and Darius knew that. There was no *for ever* for them. If there was, he wouldn't have left. No, she had said yes to this moment. A night to forget her heavy heart, her hurt and her anger, and to just be with the man she had been craving since he'd appeared at her front door.

Thoughts of tomorrow could wait until dawn, she thought to herself. Then her mind was wiped of any thought, all of her attention homing in on where his tongue connected with her body as he parted her with a stroke.

'Oh, *Deus*…' Her breath was ragged, the heat inside of her an inferno, and she prayed that this would never stop. Because with each stroke of his tongue she came closer to the edge, came more *alive* than she had felt in a long time. It was as if the world had lost some of its splendour the moment Darius had left, and now her vision had turned into Technicolor.

Celine shuddered as he pressed his tongue

flat against her. 'You are so exquisite,' he mumbled into her thigh before nipping at it, drawing another yelp from her that made her clasp her hands over her mouth, eyes wide.

Darius only smirked, the intent to hinder her being as silent as possible clearly written on his face. Yet he showed some mercy as he caught her eyes and said, 'Are you ready?'

The heat pulsing through her, release so close she sensed it at the edge of her mind, scrambled her brain. Only when he lowered his face again, with a hungry glint in his eyes, did Celine understand what he meant.

Sensation exploded through her as his tongue was joined by his fingers, and she stretched her arms above her. Her fingers grazed over the sheet and she reached, desperate to close her hand around the pillow before Darius could make her...

Celine grasped the edge of the pillow between two fingers and pulled it down, slamming it down on her face as release barrelled through her with such intensity that even the soft cushion wasn't enough to fully absorb her scream.

Darius kept stroking her through the aftermath of her orgasm, and when she dared to lower the pillow again to gulp for air he stood in front of her with a devilish grin that squeezed her heart.

'I missed you,' she said, giving voice to the ache in her chest and the warmth in her body that was partially caused by what he had done, but also because of who he was—what he meant to her, back then and now.

The mischievous grin softened at her words, and the look in his eyes almost broke her heart all over again. The traitorous words hung on her lips, words she had said so many times and wanted to shout them again, but knew she couldn't—not when she still felt the pain of the scars he had left with his disappearance. Not when there was so much at stake between them. This night was all they could have.

This moment was so perfect Darius never wanted it to end. He stood in front of her and drank in all her naked glory.

He'd missed her too, and over the last weeks this had become abundantly clear to him. When he had still been trapped in a web of lies, he'd had to justify his abandonment to himself to not crack under the guilt, and once he'd seen what mistakes he'd made he didn't dare to intrude back into her life—not when he was certain that she would have moved on.

But as Darius climbed into bed with his wife

the realisation struck that he had never stopped loving her. That throughout everything a part of his heart had remained locked behind the promises they had made to each other six years ago.

He pulled her into his arms, the soft kiss he breathed onto her lips now fuelled by passion, and a moment later she had him on his back while she straddled him. As his manhood strained against her he was cautious not to go too far and he reached for the drawer of his nightstand and pulled out a condom.

Celine watched with hungry eyes as he rolled it down, and as his hands settled back on her hips she leaned forward, kissing him.

Bright stars appeared in front of his vision as he dipped into her wet heat, the feel of her exactly like he remembered and yet so different at the same time. Her tongue darted into his mouth, her moans filling his ears as he held onto her hips, guiding her—or rather letting her guide him.

His breath mingled with hers as she bent down for another kiss, and Darius wrapped his arms around her, pulling himself up. His hand slipped between them to find the bundle of nerves to stroke in tandem with his thrusts.

Celine's breathing grew heavier, her breasts pushing against his chest. She let out a low moan when he dipped his head down and sucked one of her nipples into his mouth, rolling it over his tongue.

'Darius, please…' she huffed, her fingers clawing into his shoulders. 'Please, please, I am so…close.'

She waved her hand at something behind him, and he stilled momentarily, a grin spreading over his lips as he understood. Grabbing her by the waist, he pulled Celine off him and then flipped her around so she was lying on her stomach. Her hands were already clasping the pillow, her chest heaving with each breath, and he knew her next orgasm was in sight.

So was his, but he couldn't resist taking a moment to stroke his hands down her back, her muscles smooth and defined, no doubt from how physically demanding her work was. A burden he planned on sharing with her going forward. How they would go about it, he wasn't sure, but he knew that he would move mountains to make it work with her this time around.

'Darius!' Her voice was a mixture of a plea and a demand, her tone surging straight to his groin, and as he reached around her to put his finger back where it belonged, he thrust into her again. Her hips moved in rhythm with him, her front pressing against his hand in a frantic chase to the finish line.

Darius heard the drawn-out moan swallowed by the pillow just as he felt her convulse around him. The second he rolled off her, he snaked his arms around her and pulled her back to his chest. He placed a kiss on the back of her neck, catching a whiff of her scent as he nestled his nose into her hair.

This moment was pure and undiluted perfection, he thought as he closed his eyes and relished the warmth of her body and the silken feel of her skin against his.

CHAPTER NINE

THE REST OF the week in São Paulo went by in a flash and by the end of it Darius had conjured up an image of harmonious family life that Celine so desperately wanted to believe. Everything she had ever wanted from her marriage with him was right there—days spent with their daughter, nights spent with each other, and everything in between filled with joy and laughter.

But she knew it wasn't real. Knew it because though she enjoyed being by his side, relished every touch and still shivered with need hours after they had made love to each other, she held her breath for the pain to catch up with her. And that was the big red flag in their relationship she couldn't ignore.

She wasn't relaxed, at least not entirely, always preparing herself for the inevitable end to the whirlwind rekindling of their attraction to each other. Attraction, *not* love. That was something she reminded herself of every time she fell asleep in his arms, his warmth surrounding her to a point where she could almost imagine a life like this.

Their lives were not the same, the paths they had taken too different. How could she leave Maria and her work at the charity behind when she owed so much to her sister? She wasn't free to leave Santarém, whether she wanted to or not.

Nothing about this week had been rooted in reality, and they'd have to talk about it. Something that was made infinitely harder as Darius hauled her into his arms every time they were alone. Though they hadn't really spoken about any of this, neither of them wanting to disturb this fragile framework they had created, they had at least come to a silent understanding that they would keep their hands to themselves in front of Nina.

'Are you all packed up?' Celine asked her daughter.

They sat around the dining table, with Darius having surprised her once more by whipping up a lavish breakfast for them for their last morning in São Paulo. Their plane was leaving later in the afternoon to take them to Manaus, where they would catch the next flight back to Santarém.

Nina nodded as she bit into the churro on her plate, the dusting sugar clinging to her mouth. 'Do we have to leave so soon?' she asked, the sadness in her voice stabbing at Celine's chest.

'You know Mummy has to work, *filha*. But we will be back soon, and Pai can come visit us too.'

A chill pooled in her stomach at the thought of having to return home, of leaving this perfect week of affection and fun behind her to return to what her life had been like before Darius had come back—even though she *knew* that this was the only way.

Nothing had changed that would make her believe this time around would be different. They were still the same people, and attraction could not sustain their relationship for long. The trust was too far gone, the risk of hurting Nina in the process too great. The best thing to do was to move on from this week, treating it as the closure she had wanted for them both. They might still be sexually compatible, but their past failings clearly showed that they were not meant for each other—no matter how wrong that thought felt.

But her daughter's words reminded her of another conversation they needed to have. One Celine was actually looking forward to among all the complicated emotions they had woven around each other. She reached her hand out and laid it on Nina's arm.

'Isn't there something you wanted to ask before we leave?' she prompted her daughter, who looked at her with a puzzled expression. 'Remember what you asked me before bedtime?'

Her heart had melted when Nina had whispered the question into her ear, both excited and anxious to deepen the relationship she had with her father—something that didn't really help with Celine's own complex feelings, but she would never discourage her daughter because of her own struggles.

'Oh, right…' Nina looked up to Darius, who wore a curious look on his face. 'Can I call you Pai like Mummy does?'

'Can you…?' Darius's voice trailed off, shock rounding his eyes at the question, and Celine had to bite back a laugh.

When Nina had asked her that question she'd decided that they should all have a conversation about it. When she'd first introduced her husband to their daughter, she had decided not to force or even encourage Nina to call him Pai. That needed to be something that came from Nina herself whenever she felt ready to call him by that title.

What she hadn't expected was the confidence and nonchalance her daughter showed when she asked—free from the emotional weight that came with such a question. No, all of the emotions landed on Darius's shoulders when he hadn't expected it. The mist in his eyes as he processed her question was the sweetest heartbreak Celine had ever experienced, and she had to reel in her own reaction. This moment was between father and daughter.

'I… Yes, of course, *princesa*. I would love nothing more,' he finally said, his voice strained with the held-back emotions she sensed bubbling beneath the surface of his words.

'Okay! Now, Pai… Will you come to the dog show next weekend?' Nina asked, pulling Celine out of her thoughts.

But, before she could say anything, Darius asked, 'Dog show?'

'Tia Maria's charity has a dog show where the dogs of the village compete for prizes. We get to pet all the doggies.' Nina's eyes sparkled. Even though she was often surrounded by very exotic and sometimes rare animals, her daughter preferred dogs over anything else.

The annual dog show their charity organised was one of her favourite times. Celine also had flat-out forgotten about it, her mind too preoccupied with the sudden appearance of her estranged husband—and the resurgence of unwanted emotions that were doing their best to cloud her mind.

'It's quite the affair in Santarém,' Celine added when she saw his brow rise. She wasn't sure if she would have invited him—had she even remembered. But, knowing how much it meant to Nina, she couldn't not invite him. 'You should come if your schedule allows. I know it's far, but it's a bit of a family tradition that we are all there.'

Truth be told, though she wanted Nina to see Darius often, she had been hoping for a break to cool her nerves around him. They had yet to discuss what had transpired this week, neither of them seemingly daring to say anything that might break whatever spell they had woven together.

Say yes to me, to us.

The words echoed in her mind, the rawness in his voice, as if his life had depended on her saying yes, etched into her memory. But were they both aware of what they had agreed to? Celine wasn't sure at this point. There was no way he'd thought they would try again, was there?

'I'd love to come,' he said, his smile, though

directed at their daughter, sending sparks raining down her spine.

Nina smiled from ear to ear, the excitement of having her father at the dog show clear to anyone who looked at her, and Celine's heart twisted inside her chest. She wouldn't ruin this for her daughter by getting involved with Darius. Whatever had happened here in São Paulo would have to stay here, the memories of his touch all she would take with her.

Celine hadn't been joking when she had said that the dog show in Santarém was quite the affair. Darius sat on a bench some distance away from all the action as the Dias family set up everything for the dog show, with villagers and their pooches ready to help.

He'd asked several times if he could be of assistance, but Celine and Maria had waved him off multiple times—and ended up banishing him to this bench so he was no longer in the way.

'Ah, I see you got exiled as well. Welcome to the club.' Darius twisted around to see a man approaching and sitting down next to him. His face was familiar. He'd been the one to pick up Bruna after he had sutured her wound.

'You're Maria's husband?' he asked, and

the man laughed before stretching his hand out to him.

'I used to be Rafael Pedro but nowadays "Maria's husband" is more popular,' he said as they shook hands.

'Darius Delgado,' he replied, and Rafael nodded, clearly aware of who he was.

'My reputation precedes me?' he asked with a smirk, earning him another laugh from Rafael.

'Don't worry, it's probably not as bad as you think. Though the sisters are tight, Maria is the one who needs Celine to talk her through things—not so much the other way around.' He shot Darius a knowing look. 'Doesn't mean they don't talk.'

Darius sighed, a heaviness settling into his chest that had been haunting him for the last week. Communication with Celine had been sparse, most of their messages revolving around Nina and the logistics of his visit. He knew that before he left to go back to São Paulo tomorrow, they would need to sit down and talk about a schedule. They'd been lucky that for the last few weeks he'd been off work with the Brazilian football league on break, but that was changing now and he wouldn't have the freedom to stay for as long as he wanted.

Though, instead of talking about schedules

and flights, what Darius really wanted to do was to ask her to move to São Paulo with him. Move in *with* him, resume the life they had been living last week. The time they had spent together had been a vision of the future—or rather the present if they had made different choices in the past.

'So, is this where they banish the useless husbands to?' he asked in a joking tone that matched the slight smile he saw on the other man's face.

'Pretty much. Though, like most of the charity work, this is Maria's brainchild and poor Celine gets roped into helping her. It's a strange situation that both are in.'

Darius's ears sharpened at that. Rafael was striking a conversational tone, but his words were weighed down with a meaning that went beyond the surface level. This man was trying to tell him something.

'What situation is that?' he asked point-blank.

'The charity is Maria's passion—has been since the day she was old enough to help her parents at the rescue. But the same isn't true for Celine. She seems to be happy to let Maria make the decisions and be the face of the charity while pursuing her own work with the farmers,' he said, his eyes drifting towards the two women, who were setting up the table with the prizes—several bags of dog food and a mountain of different toys.

Darius only grunted at the information, comparing it to his own observations. Celine had told him that as well, and hearing this hadn't surprised him. Though they were always pretty tight, their passions differed, with Maria far more invested in the family's rescue operations.

'She didn't come here of her own choice but out of necessity,' Darius said, fighting to keep the growl from his tone. Dwelling on his mistakes in the past would not help him now as he was trying to figure out where they stood in their relationship.

She had said yes, had given him everything he'd been yearning for since he'd seen her again, and that week together had been nothing short of a fantasy come to life. Had she understood what he'd been trying to tell her? That he wanted them to try and save this marriage?

He shot Rafael a sideways glance. Was that what this man was trying to tell him?

Sensing his gaze, Rafael nodded. 'Yes…she needed help, and back then her parents, her brother and Maria were ready to support her with whatever she needed. I think this has instilled a sense of obligation in her, a loyalty to her sister. Maria has been relying less and less on Celine to run her charity, but keeps pulling her in—because she, too, doesn't want to give the impression that she's pushing her sister out just because I'm here now.'

Rafael raised his hand towards the two women. Maria had moved on to the middle of the park and was trying to get Alexander, the family's Great Dane, to engage with the obstacle course they had created. Nina and her cousin Mirabel were at her heels, laughing and clapping as the dog climbed up one of the ramps. Celine, however, stood a few paces back with her arms crossed in front of her.

'She doesn't want to be involved, but she can't say no because she thinks she owes Maria.' The thought sank into his consciousness, dropping far below the surface and settling in an uncomfortable pinch in the pit of his stomach. What exactly did that mean for them? Would she consider leaving?

Rafael nodded and said, 'Maria, on the other hand, feels obliged to involve her because it's the family legacy. For the longest time it's just been the two of them, raising their kids on their own.'

Darius turned his head, looking into the

other man's hazel eyes. 'What's your point, Pedro?'

The man frowned, his eyes drifting back towards where both of their wives stood. 'My point is they are so stuck in this routine, and in assuming that what they are doing is what the other sister wants, that they cannot see a way out. Not without someone presenting a new…option.'

Darius followed his gaze, his eyes locking into Celine's at a distance. Her expression remained veiled for a few heartbeats, then she smiled at him with a small wave of her hand.

An option? Like coming back to São Paulo with him?

'I don't know if the option that I have is what she wants,' Darius said, his heart twisting at the mere thought of rejection.

But hadn't she said yes last week? He'd asked her to choose them, and every night she had ended up in his room, his bed, his arms.

Next to him, Rafael shrugged. 'I have my suspicions around that, but Celine is the only one who can tell you. She can't pick an option that she doesn't know about.'

Darius's eyes rounded, his head snapping back to Rafael as the words sank in. An option she didn't know about? He looked back towards Celine, then at Nina, who was holding Alexander's lead and encouraging him to jump through a hoop. Laughter echoed across the park when the Great Dane lay down instead, placing his large head on top of his paws with a yawn.

That was what he needed to talk about with Celine—he had to tell her how he felt, how his affection and love for her had never stopped but only slept, waiting for the right moment to reawaken.

The choice was hers—but he had to make sure she knew that he *was* a choice.

The turnout for the dog show this year was a lot higher than any of the other events Celine remembered—and she believed a large part of that had to do with the social media following their charity had attracted after a video of Rafael rescuing a mother cat and her kittens went viral.

Celine was glad of it as more people meant more donations, but she wasn't one to enjoy the spotlight. So, instead of being in there with Maria and the villagers, Celine chose to hover on the sidelines of the spectacle, observing instead of getting involved. Something she had done more and more with the arrival of Rafael and his taking up a larger role in the rescue.

The highlight of her day so far had turned

out to be Darius and seeing him interact with Nina. Once the dog show had begun, Nina had taken her father by the hand and walked him through the family history of every single dog that was on the roster. And Darius had listened to her patiently, asked questions to keep her talking and interacted with the dogs she pointed out as if they were part of the audience rather than the show.

Not that the show was particularly strict. They called it a dog show, but it was really more an opportunity for the community to get together and shore up some donations for the charity.

She cast her eyes around. Darius caught her attention, standing some paces away with Nina on his shoulders, and the sight brought forward a deep yearning unlike anything she had ever felt. The desire for her own family stirred in her chest. An idea that could become a reality if she dared.

But, after a week apart, their week together seemed more like a dream than reality. Was it even possible to have what they'd had last week on a long-term basis, when their lives were so far apart from each other? Celine doubted it, not when her place was here, next to her sister, who still relied on her to help with the charity.

Could she trust Darius to treat her heart with

more care this time around? Doubt remained embedded in her chest as she cast her eyes inward, believing this to be her answer. With a lump growing in her throat, she walked towards Darius. They needed to talk.

The smile he gave her as she came to a stop next to him threatened to break her resolve.

'You two having fun?' she asked, and smiled when Nina answered her question with a vigorous nod.

'Freya is still so agile,' Nina said, pointing at the dog now climbing a ramp.

'Anabel keeps her well exercised.' Freya's owner, Anabel, was walking alongside her dog, giving her directions through the obstacle course.

They watched the show in silence, Celine drifting closer to Darius. Even through the crowds comprised of both humans and animals she was still able to pick up his scent— the smell of spice so delicious she wasn't sure she would be able to give it up.

'Will you be there for dinner? I think we should talk,' she asked Darius, earning herself a sideways glance.

'I was about to say the same thing,' he replied, his expression not letting her see what thoughts lay beneath the surface.

'What do you—'

The screeching of tyres ripped through the air, all heads turning as a car lost control on the road running parallel to the little park. It spun around, smoke rising from where the tyres tried to grip the road, and then the side of the car crashed into the iron gate that marked the entrance to the park. Shouts of fright mingled with the barking of several dogs, everyone frozen into place as they watched the accident happen—everyone except Darius.

His hands closed around Nina's waist and he pulled her off his shoulders, setting her down on the grass. 'I have to go help them,' he said.

'I'll go with you, maybe you'll need some help,' Celine said.

He nodded, then pointed at the judges' table. 'Nina, go stand with your aunt and uncle. You'll be safe there, okay?'

Nina nodded, eyes wide in shock, then she ran over to where Maria was half standing from her chair, ready to intervene as well. Celine waved her sister off, then turned and followed Darius as he walked towards the car.

The driver's side had hit the iron gate, the car bending inwards where it had suffered the impact, and through the windscreen she could see two unconscious figures in the front seats.

'I'll have to check both of them through the passenger side since we can't move them safely.' Darius circled around to the other side of the car and pulled the handle. The door did not budge. He whispered a curse under his breath, his eyes casting about. 'Do we have any tools around to help us open the door? If we wait for them to wake up it might already be too late.'

'Oh, I have something,' she mumbled, to herself as much as to Darius, and pulled her key chain from the small bag hanging from her shoulder, unclipping one of the tools hanging from it and giving it to him.

The tool was made out of purple plastic, one side sloping down and the other side capped off with a black stopper. He took it in his hand, turning it around once. A line appeared between his brows, and he looked at her in a silent question. Celine took the tool back, uncapping it, and held it against the back window. Then she pushed a button on the side of the tool, releasing a metal pin.

Spider cracks appeared around the tool, webbing throughout the window. She looked back at Darius as she said, 'This is a tool to cut belts and break car windows in case I ever get stuck in a car.'

'I'll have to ask you about why you carry this around with you later on,' he said, then watched as she pushed against the window with some force, the glass giving in under her hand and spilling onto the back seat.

Celine reached through the window to the front of the passenger side, pulling at the pin to unlock the door. She breathed out a sigh of relief when Darius pulled the door open, kneeling in front of the still unconscious passenger. He held his ear close to her face, then pulled back.

'She's still breathing but not conscious,' he said, then stepped back to look at the driver, whose head was moving from one side to the other, seemingly conscious but not reacting to what was happening. 'We can't pull them out until the emergency services arrive to secure their necks and spines in case of any injuries.'

Celine nodded, then dialled the emergency number, the call going though almost immediately. She described the scene in front of her, approximating the age of the patients, then turned to Darius, who had just re-emerged from the vehicle, to ask if he had any more details to add.

'Both patients are breathing, one of them conscious and complaining of chest pain,' he said as she held the phone to his ear, then he nodded as the call disconnected. 'An ambulance is too far out so they are bringing in a helicopter.'

A low moan brought their attention back to the car. The patient on the passenger side had opened her eyes, staring dead ahead as she muttered something that neither of them could understand.

A pin on the passenger's sweater caught her attention. It was an enamel pin with three black dots on a yellow background. 'She's blind,' Celine said to Darius, who followed her gaze to the pin.

He went on his knees, leaning forward to place his ear right in front of her mouth. Then he looked at Celine over his shoulder, wearing a confused expression. 'She says Bella was with her.'

'Bella?' They both looked at the driver, who held his hand to his chest, a dangerous-sounding cough shaking his body.

Darius let out a low curse before leaning back into the vehicle. '*Senhor*, try to take deep, calm breaths. I suspect one of your lungs has collapsed, making it hard to breathe. The medevac is en route.'

As if to underline his words, the faint sounds of a faraway helicopter echoed over the constant mutter of the crowd that was standing several paces away, thankfully letting Darius do his work.

'Bella is…' the man tried to press out, then another coughing fit interrupted him.

Celine gasped when the pieces clicked into place. 'Bella is her service dog!'

And she had broken the window inward, right on top of where Bella had probably been on the floor.

She rushed to the rear door, pulling at the mechanical lock then yanking the door open. A quiet whine crept into her ears, too high to hear over the commotion. On the floor lay a Golden Retriever, Bella, with her ears close to her skull and her tongue flicking over her mouth nervously. The hi-vis vest was still attached to her body, her harness thrust to the other side of the car.

'Hey gorgeous,' Celine said in a low voice, the high-pitched whine coming from the dog a clear sign of distress. 'Let me check if you're hurt.'

She leaned in and palpated the dog's legs, stomach and back as well as she could from her position. 'I don't feel any bumps or abnormalities. Let's see if you can walk.' Celine grabbed the dog by her vest and pulled, hoping that the strict training of a service dog would kick in and she would move despite her fear.

Bella did so, and when she stepped onto the floor she immediately raised her left hind leg, keeping her weight off it as she stepped forward. Celine went back onto her knees, casting her eyes skyward. The sound of helicopter blades filled the air now, its arrival imminent. She wrapped her arms around Bella, lifting the dog with a grunt, putting her down in front of the passenger side door.

She looked over her shoulder, searching the crowd, and lifted her hand when she locked eyes with Rafael, waving him towards her.

'Can she understand me?' she asked Darius as she looked at the woman, who was still staring ahead without any further reaction.

He nodded, so Celine said, 'I freed Bella from the car. She has an injury on her leg, but she seems otherwise well. I'm a vet, so I will take her to my clinic to get treatment. Once that's done, I'll drive her to the hospital.'

The woman's eyes rounded and, sensing her owner's distress, Bella limped forward and wedged her head in her hands. 'I can't be without her,' the woman said, voice hoarse.

'They can't treat her leg at the hospital, *senhora*. Please trust me with her, and I will return her to you as soon as she is patched up. She's limping and in pain, let me help her.' The sounds of the helicopter had swelled to a loud roar that swept over the village, and when Celine looked back she saw it descending from the sky and landing on a free patch of grass a few metres away from them.

Rafael appeared behind her, crouching down next to her. 'This dog needs help?' he asked, immediately understanding the situation.

Celine nodded, thankful to have her brother-in-law nearby. 'I can treat her, but I can't carry her all the way back.'

Rafael pushed both of his arms under the dog, lifting her off the ground, and nodded towards the exit. Their clinic was luckily only a short walk away. Celine hesitated, looking at Darius, who got to his feet as two people hopped out of the helicopter.

'Are you okay here?' she asked, a strange part of her unwilling to leave him alone, even though she knew her help was needed elsewhere.

'I'll find out what hospital they'll go to so we can drive the dog once she is fit to go,' he replied, and that little word *we* made her heart skip a beat.

'I can stay if you need me. Rafael will be okay.' She didn't know why she had offered that, some impulse inside of her not wanting to be away from Darius.

He, too, seemed to have picked up on the subtext in her words, for he put his hand on her cheek and brushed a light kiss onto her lips, his eyes filled with affection. Her stomach twisted at the sight, her heart beating faster. He should not be looking at her like that—like they had a future.

'Go take care of Bella. I will be there as soon as I've seen the paramedics off.'

He dropped his hand to his side, then strode towards the two figures scurrying over from the medevac.

CHAPTER TEN

TEN MINUTES AFTER its arrival the helicopter had been airborne again, taking the two car crash victims to a nearby city. Darius had noted the name of the hospital and looked up the distance—a two-hour drive. Something to worry about once Celine had assessed the dog and how soon it would be able to travel.

After the helicopter lifted off a murmur had rippled through the crowd, who had all turned to look, some even holding their phones in front of them as if they were filming. Thankfully, Maria had shooed the crowd away after a few minutes, handing his daughter back to him and sending him to the house while she dealt with the unsettled villagers. A task he'd been all too happy to leave to her.

Hours had passed since then, enough time that Darius had made the decision to have dinner with Nina before putting her to bed.

Now he stood at the window, looking out

at the clinic, where one lonely light was on. He'd seen Rafael leave almost two hours ago, making him think Celine had decided to treat the dog herself.

Darius's nerves were stretched thin, his heart beating inside his throat as he went over the words he wanted to tell her today. The ones he had said so many years ago, had repeated many times over before they'd got married.

A kernel of fear had nestled itself inside his heart this morning, growing larger with each passing minute that he waited for her. She had asked to speak to him tonight, though nothing in her expression had told him if it was the same thing he wanted to talk about.

They still hadn't agreed on how often he would come to visit, or if Nina would be permitted to visit him in São Paulo without her mother. Those were important things they needed to agree on.

But, equally, they hadn't spoken about what had happened between them in São Paulo— how they had slept with each other every single night. Celine had spoken of closure, of getting over what they had lost and moving on with their lives. He'd asked her to choose him, choose them, and he'd meant it. These had not been cheap words he'd spoken to get her into bed.

Darius was still in love with his wife, and tonight he would tell her.

He straightened his back when the light turned off, holding his breath as he saw a figure emerging from the building several minutes later, walking towards the house. A moment later, the door handle twisted and Celine stepped inside, looking as tired as he felt.

She looked at him, eyes wide in surprise. 'You waited for me?'

Darius furrowed his brow at her astonishment. 'I didn't think I should let Nina sleep here on her own.'

Celine's eyes darted around, scanning the kitchen and then the living room, stopping to inspect every trace he'd left in her house. 'You were alone with her?'

The sharp edge in her voice drove straight through his chest and into his heart, spearing physical pain through his body. After the last few weeks together, after what had happened between them in São Paulo, she *still* didn't trust him?

'Of course I was alone with her. She is my child, Celine.' The hurt her question had caused him wove itself through his tone, the words coming out in a low growl.

Celine clenched her jaw, a deep line appearing between her brows as she levelled a stare at him. 'I left her with Maria for a reason.'

'Your sister was too busy handling the fall-out at the dog show, so she handed me *my* daughter to take her home.' Darius couldn't believe what he was hearing from Celine. What more would he have to do to show her he was serious about being a part of his child's life—that he would never let anything happen to her?

'I told you I'm not comfortable with you being alone with her at the moment. Why would you disrespect this one request?' She let out a bitter laugh, the sound so twisted that he could hardly recognise her. 'Oh, right, you don't take promises very seriously. That's on me for forgetting that.'

His stomach twisted, the pain lancing through him intensifying as her words sank in. Her barb struck true, hitting him in the one place she knew would hurt him beyond anything else. The need to turn around and leave bubbled up in him, turn his back before he could say anything unkind in return. He closed his eyes, taking a few deep breaths before facing her again.

He was no longer the man who would run from his wife, no matter what she had to say to him. Though the hope that had grown bigger and bigger each time she had returned to his room last week wilted at her harsh words—at the hurt that lay beneath them.

'Celine…this was an emergency. You, of all people, should know that. I didn't take her because I wanted to go against your wishes. I took her because there was chaos at the park, and *I am her father.*' His last words came out thick with the hurt her words had caused him.

But from the way Celine crossed her arms in front of her, she wasn't seeing it his way. How was he supposed to have the conversation he'd been planning in his head? The fear clawing at him exploded through his chest, almost robbing him of breath.

If she didn't trust him alone with their daughter, what were the chances that she would invite him back to be her husband? Darius knew he had to say it, even though he saw his plans for their future together crumbling before him. He would regret it if he didn't. He took two steps forward, closing the space between them.

'The moment you told me about Nina my life changed for ever. A place inside my heart unlocked, flooding with joy and fear alike as I became a father in that moment—knowing I'm now responsible for her life, her wellbeing and her happiness.' His hand went up to his chest, clutching his heart. 'Even six years late, there isn't a greater gift you could have given me, Cee.'

Celine's lips parted to say something, a protest, going by the gleam in her eyes, but he continued. 'I know I hurt you, and I can't change that. But I showed you at every turn in the last few weeks that I *am* a changed man. I learned from my mistakes, and I'm not letting them get in my way any more.'

He heaved in a deep breath, steeling himself for the one thing he had to say to lay it all out—and then the ball would be in her court.

'Celine...' His voice was thick with the joy and pain that combined themselves into a deadly cocktail inside his heart. 'I love you. What else do I have to do to show you I've changed—that I'm worthy of your trust?'

Celine's eyes rounded, his words driving the air out of her lungs. The words she had been dreading to hear—*longing* to hear in the safety of her dreams—crossed his lips and were now floating in the space between them. Along with the question Celine had been too afraid to address.

A part of her knew that her reaction to him being alone with Nina was unnecessary, caused by the fierce protectiveness she felt towards her daughter. She did what she had to do to protect Nina, to make sure Darius coming back into her life was not something that she would come to regret—that would cause her any heartache. If that meant Celine was the one who had to bear the heartache then this was a price she was willing to pay.

'I can't trust you, Darius. I can't *love* you, not after everything that happened,' she said, her voice shaking with the pain her own words were inflicting on her.

'Why not?'

The defeat in his face almost undid her, tears she quickly blinked away threatening to fall.

'Because you left when I needed you the most. That your reasons were noble doesn't help with the scars that your actions left on me.' Her lower lip trembled as she struggled to keep her voice steady. 'Coming back and proving your trustworthiness when things are easy is not enough to show me you've changed.'

The words tasted bitter in her mouth as she questioned the truth of her own argument. She meant what she said, but the origin of her words was a place of fear and hurt—a place she shouldn't be making permanent decisions from. Yet that was all that was in her right now, raging like an inferno as his declaration of love rippled through her.

'In order to prove to you I have changed I need to find you when you're down?' he asked, incredulity lacing his words.

She swallowed the lump in her throat as she forced the next words out of her mouth. 'There is nothing you can do to change my mind.'

Silence stretched between them, and a part of Celine prayed he would leave—the way he had left six years ago. She wanted to curl up into a ball and let the agony of this moment settle in her.

I love you. The words echoed through her, finding purchase in her own heart, where the words were reflected back at him. But she couldn't say it, wouldn't risk it. Not when Nina had finally got the chance to have her father in her life.

Celine's feelings would always come second.

Darius's face showed the pain her words caused in him, and she had to clench her teeth to stop herself from reaching out to wrap him in her arms. He swallowed, then he said, 'Then why did you say yes?'

Her breath stuttered in her chest, the moment when she had given in to him appearing in her mind's eye—a memory that hurt as much as it soothed her. Because for those seven days their lives had been perfect, their minds and bodies and hearts in sync, and, for a brief moment, Celine had believed that she could do this. Could have her husband back.

But that had been nothing more than an idle fantasy.

'I didn't think you meant it when you asked me to say yes to us. We were both caught up in the moment. After what happened between us at Juliana's farm, I thought we both just needed to…get things out of our system.' The truth was blurred though, her words only partly ringing true in her ears. She had wanted to believe that he'd meant what he said, but that also struck so much fear in her heart that she'd immediately retreated—treating their week together as just sex.

'I meant it…' he whispered, his words trailing off and stretching into silence between them. 'I meant all of it. Every kiss, every touch. Everything I did was to show you I'm here for good.'

She took another trembling breath, shaking her head. 'I think it's best that we focus on our relationship as co-parents.'

Darius's eyes shuttered at her words, the pain she'd seen but a second ago gone, replaced with a stony expression that wouldn't let her see what lay behind. He silently stalked past her, stepping into the kitchen and grabbing the stack of papers she had shoved between the fridge and the microwave, intending to deal with them later.

He dropped the stack onto the kitchen table, and her heart sank when she realised they were their divorce papers. Then he grabbed the pen that hung from a magnet on the fridge door. The rustling of paper filled the silence between them, the only interruption the scratching of a pen on paper. After what felt an eternity, Darius stood up straight again, putting the pen back onto the fridge.

Celine took a step back when he grabbed the papers and pushed them into her hands.

'There you go, Celine. You are officially done with me,' he said, some of the pain slipping through his icy exterior. 'I'll be in touch about Nina.'

And then he walked through the door and out of her life again, the gap he was leaving yawning open within her.

CHAPTER ELEVEN

DARIUS'S HEART TWISTED inside his chest as he pressed the call button, knowing that in a few seconds he would see—

Celine's face appeared on his phone, a searing pain stabbing through him at the sight of his lost love. Her mouth twitched when she saw him, as if she was fighting down a smile.

He'd returned to São Paulo to lick his wounds and patch himself back up—a task that took a lot more effort than he had energy for. His only relief from it was his daily phone calls with his daughter. Though they came with the drawback of having to see Celine first, constantly reopening the wound.

'Hey, Darius,' she said, the tone of her voice unusually lacklustre.

He opened his mouth to say something, to ask her how she was or what she had been up to, *anything* to bring some kind of normality back into their relationship as parents.

But, before he could find the right words, Celine's phone twisted and Nina popped up on his screen, a small smile on her face.

'*Hola, mi princesa hermosa,*' he said, her face easing the dark clouds gathering in his head.

'Hi, Dad! I'm at my *tia*'s house.' She grabbed the phone from where Celine had put it, panning the camera around to show him the interior of Maria's house—including Rafael, who lay on the couch with his baby sleeping on his chest.

Darius glanced at the clock on his phone, then he asked, 'Are you over there for dinner?'

'I'm having a sleepover with Mirabel because Mummy is working...' His ears sharpened as her words trailed off, his daughter's voice gaining a strange quality.

'What's wrong, princess? You usually like sleepovers with your cousin.'

'Mummy has been working a lot lately, and I miss having her home.' She paused, her big brown eyes almost round as she stared down at the phone screen. 'I miss you here too.'

Tears suddenly spilled over her cheeks, and Darius's heart shattered again into the thousand pieces it had been in when he had left Santarém to come back to São Paulo. Helplessness flooded him as his daughter sobbed, her words no longer intelligible.

'*Bebê*, don't cry. I'm going to come and visit you in two weeks and we'll have lots of fun together, I promise.' Nina's tears continued and, a moment later, Maria popped into the frame, scooping Nina into her arms.

'Hang on a second, Darius,' she said, and he watched helplessly as she cut the time with his daughter short.

The angle of the camera changed, giving him a view of the ceiling. Then a familiar face appeared on the screen. Rafael smiled at him, a sympathetic look on his face.

'*Oi, cunhado,*' he said, then adjusted the phone so Darius could see the baby lying on his chest.

His choice of word sent a stab through him. 'Brother-in-law no more, Pedro. I signed the divorce papers before I left.'

Rafael chuckled as if he had just made a funny joke, and Darius's temper flared. Wasn't it enough that his daughter was crying for him without him being able to do something about it? Now this man was laughing at what was the most miserable time in his life?

'Sure, if you want to reduce it to a piece of paper, I guess we can agree,' he said, and

Darius thought he saw a flash of regret in Rafael's eyes.

'Listen… I don't know what Celine told you two about what happened, but I honestly don't want to get into any of that. All I want is to talk to Nina,' he gritted out through his teeth, reminding himself to stay calm. Maria and Rafael had nothing to do with his foul mood, so he shouldn't let it show so much.

'She'd rather stay with you than here with us. It seems she got used to having you around.' The baby—Sam, if he remembered the name right—coughed, her eyes opening for a fraction of a second before fluttering shut again. Rafael's hand came down on her back, rubbing up and down.

Envy came out of nowhere, spearing through him with a flashing heat that left him without words. Before he'd gone to Santarém to talk to Celine—to ask her not to divorce him just yet—he hadn't known what was missing in his life, but now that he knew what having his wife and daughter felt like it was as if he was walking through a world of muted colour. *He* wanted to be the man to lie on the couch with his sleeping baby on his chest, and it didn't make sense to him that he wasn't. Not when he had done everything he could.

Rafael seemed to read his thoughts from the

expressions flitting over his face, for he gave him a crooked smile. 'Here's the thing, Delgado. I was in a similar position a year ago, running away from the woman I loved because I convinced myself that she would be better off without me.'

Darius straightened at that, his brow furrowing. He'd never heard that part of their story before. Whenever Celine had spoken about them, it sounded like love at first sight, with both being exactly what the other one needed—the way it had been with them when they'd first met.

Except Darius wasn't running away. Sure, he'd left, but not without asking her to reconsider. Not without telling her how he felt.

'I didn't run,' he said, reinforcing that thought, but Rafael only chuckled at that.

'Then why aren't you here fighting for her?'

His eyes widened at that question as he struggled to come up with an answer. Fight for her? But she…

'She asked me to leave. What else was I supposed to do?'

'Did you give her the choice to come with you?'

'I…' Darius's voice trailed off as he cast his thoughts inward, remembering that fateful night that now lay a few weeks back. He'd been so sure of his feelings back then, convinced that she felt the same. Had been devastated to find out she didn't. A lot of things had been said that night, most of them hurtful, but...

'No, I didn't. She came back after treating the dog and when she realised I had been alone with Nina she accused me of disrespecting her request. Things escalated from there, and then I...told her I loved her.' Hadn't that been clear enough in his intentions?

Rafael nodded, the smile gone and replaced with an expression of deep sympathy. Whatever had gone on between him and Maria had been bad enough for him to understand his pain. Though even then they had got to the other side, were living a life he *dreamed* of living.

'How?' he asked, completely out of context, yet his brother-in-law somehow knew what he meant.

'I fought for her. Our lovely Dias sisters have been through a lot, Delgado. First Celine was forced to come back to Santarém so your daughter would have a family, then their brother almost doomed the charity to financial ruin with his decision, abandoning his daughter to their care.' He paused when his baby hiccupped, gently patting her back. 'All of their experiences makes them fiercely protective, and they will...test you. Unknowingly, but they do.'

Darius stayed quiet, staring at the man on his screen as he considered his words, when Rafael added, 'Give her the choice to come with you. She loves you too. Anyone with eyes knows that. But she's not someone to walk towards the unknown. Celine likes to have a plan.'

Darius laughed at that—at the truth that smacked him in the face. Celine had *always* been a planner. He'd seen it first-hand so many times during their university days. Though he had told her he loved her, he had not given her a choice like Rafael had suggested.

'Let me ask you the same question that a friend of mine asked me a year ago when I was on the brink of giving up on Maria. What would happen if you showed up now and painted a picture of your life together? How would it be?'

There was a lot of history in Rafael's love story he didn't know, and a part of him wanted to dig deeper into that, but now was not the time. His gaze drifted around the room, imagining what his apartment would look like if they were here with him.

His spare room would become Nina's room,

while Celine would sleep in his bed every night—wake up next to him every day. There would be a space for Alexander in the corner of the living room, where the sun glowed in the morning to warm the old Great Dane. He'd be off to work at the stadium, and Celine… She could have the freedom to pursue the veterinary work she was passionate about without having to worry about her sister needing her.

Didn't she want to break free of that, anyway? Every time they had spoken about it, she had said as much.

'I have to go,' Darius mumbled as the pieces clicked into place.

She had said no because she didn't have all the information—didn't know what she could choose. Celine would never choose the unknown when she believed her responsibilities would tie her to Santarém. But that was because both sisters were so used to relying on each other, they couldn't imagine either of them not *wanting* that.

Rafael shot him a big grin. 'Ah, I know that expression all too well. See you in a bit, Delgado.' He raised his hand in a short wave, then the call disconnected.

Darius jumped to his feet, his eyes drifting to the overnight bag that he had never unpacked after getting back to São Paulo—as if he'd known he'd be needing it soon.

The sun had just crept over the horizon when Celine arrived at Maria's house. A peek through the window showed no sign of the family being up, so she let herself in with the copy of their key. Toeing off her shoes, she walked down the corridor and into the open-plan kitchen, finding the space devoid of anyone—which was just as well.

Ever since Darius had left after their argument, Celine had immersed herself in her work to keep her mind from spinning out of control. The more time she spent moving, the less space to think about what he had said—what *she* had said to him. The look of hurt in his eyes was one she wouldn't forget.

Things were difficult with Nina now too. Though Darius had only been a part of her life for two months now, her daughter had got so used to having her father around that his prolonged absence was causing her to act out. With half the country between them, he could only visit every other weekend and during school breaks. With his career being the reason he had returned to Brazil in the first place, she didn't think he would give it up to come and live in the countryside—where jobs for physicians specialising in athletes were arguably obsolete.

And Celine couldn't leave either. Though the family charity was not a cause that was close to her heart, she had seen how much Maria had put into this place, had put into helping her with Nina as well when she had been a baby. There was no way she could leave her sister now, when Maria had done so much for her.

Celine shook her head, trying her best to shoo these thoughts away. She turned towards the kitchen counter, grabbing some coffee and a mug from the cupboard, and made to set the machine up. She needed to wait until the children woke up.

'Would you mind making one for me as well?'

Celine almost dropped the mug she was holding when her sister's voice filtered through the air out of nowhere.

She whirled around, scanning her surroundings, when she saw her sister's hand appear over the back of the couch. Breathing out a laugh, Celine stepped closer to the couch. Maria lay on it with her baby on her chest. Sam had her big eyes wide open, her tiny fist resting against her lips, while her sister had her hands resting on the baby's back. Dark brown circles spread under Maria's eyes as she slowly blinked the weariness away.

'Rough night?' Celine asked, circling around the couch to sit down on the other end.

'Samara is teething, which means she likes to sleep in thirty-minute increments.' Maria sighed, looking down at her baby.

Celine blew out a breath, nodding. 'Teething is not fun. Frozen chewing toys helped a lot with Nina. It supposedly feels nice on the gums.'

'How was work?' Her sister's eyes drifted closed but, from her breathing, she could tell she was still listening.

'Good. I'm making the rounds to vaccinate all the livestock that was recently born as well as some minor surgeries that I've been putting off for a while. One of Juliana's horses keeps developing an abscess in its hoof and I can't quite figure out why.' Work had been a godsend in the last weeks, keeping her out of the house and out of her head.

She'd taken on a lot more than she usually would, her need to escape her own thoughts driving her to spend long hours on the road for consultations and checkups across several farms.

Her absence seemed to have been noted by

Maria, for she said, 'I haven't seen you around in the clinic for a while.'

Guilt stabbed through Celine. She'd hoped that her busyness wouldn't be noticed, as it would lead to a lot of questions she didn't really want to answer. Though she feared if she owed anyone some answers, it was Maria. She'd been the one taking care of Nina whenever she needed to work late at night.

'I'm sorry. I'll try to be around more. I know I've been taking advantage of your kindness by leaving Nina with you while I…' Her words drifted off into nothingness, and Maria opened her eyes.

'It's not necessary, Raf and I get it,' she said, and though warmth radiated from her eyes, the words landed in her stomach like lead. 'You helped me out a lot these last few years to keep our…no, *my* dream alive. But now that you're using it as an excuse, I feel it's my duty as your sister to let you go.'

'Let me go?' The lump appearing in her throat turned her voice hoarse. The exhaustion from working all night crept into her bones, settling with a heaviness that she struggled to shake. Was this the right moment to have such a conversation?

Maria seemed to think so, for she went on. 'I know you feel you owe me a debt of gratitude and that you have an obligation to this family—to what our parents built. But…you've given enough. You don't need to let him go.'

Her weariness turned to ice as her sister said those words. 'This is about Darius? I don't want to talk about him.'

Their argument was the reason she was feeling so hollow—why she had to bury herself in work. Anything to gain a reprieve from the thought of him, of what she had walked away from.

'You chose to involve me in this by using me as an excuse. Nina cried again during her call with Darius. And don't pretend like you haven't been crying either. Why are you so set on making your lives miserable? Because he made a mistake six years ago?'

Celine leaned back as her sister rounded on her. The ferocity in her words was unexpected, so was the sting they brought to her chest. Despite her young age, Nina could sense something at odds between her parents, and she knew from her sister that she often cried because she missed him. But that wouldn't be different if she had said the words back.

'This isn't just one mistake, Maria. How would you feel if Rafael had run away after marrying you?' she asked, then cursed under her breath when a grin spread over her sister's face.

'Ah, so you remember Rafael running away after I told him I loved him. Do you also remember all the speeches you gave me about the true nature of my feelings for him?'

Celine did remember that. When Maria and Rafael had gone through their time of crisis, it had been Celine who'd pushed her sister towards the man, believing in the love story she'd seen unravel in front of her eyes. Maria had never been happier than the moments she had spent with Rafael.

But Darius wasn't coming back.

'He signed the divorce papers.'

'But you didn't send them to the lawyer.'

Another truth that sank to the bottom of her stomach, bubbling there with the rest of them and painting a picture that Celine didn't want to be confronted with—couldn't look at, for it revealed the mistake she had made that evening when Darius had told her he loved her.

She should have said that she loved him too. Her heart, her soul, every hair on her body belonged to him—had belonged to him since they'd first got together.

'I can't ask him back. How would that even work, with him living so far away? He won't want to give up his work, and I...' Her eyes widened in surprise as she realised what Maria had said, why she had told her she was no longer needed at the clinic.

Her sister swallowed, the first sign of nerves she'd seen in her since the conversation had started. 'Go home and sleep on it, Cee. I'll keep Nina here for the day. Figure out what you want—and then go get him back.'

It was a possibility she had never taken into consideration—or, rather, she had never *let* herself consider it. Because if she thought about leaving Santarém behind Darius would have had a clear shot at her heart. But fear and past rejection had clouded her mind, rendered her immobile and unable to accept that he *had* changed—and that she needed to be brave enough to trust him again.

Celine loosened a deep breath, then got to her feet. Her thoughts were still jumbled, but a plan had formed. Maria was right. She and Rafael had gone through a crisis, and it had only made their relationship stronger. She could have that too. Celine only needed to be brave.

By the time Celine pulled her car over on the street in front of her house, she was ready to book a flight to São Paulo to talk to Darius. The week they had spent together there kept replaying inside her head, the memories some of the happiest she had. What if it was time to leave, and the pain that thought caused had been one of the factors to push him away?

What if he *was* her missing piece, the person to complete her? Not the Darius she had married, but this version—the one who had to struggle before finding his way back to her? What if their timing had just been wrong?

She jumped out of her car, her strides widening as urgency bubbled up in her, when an unfamiliar car caught her attention. A man stood next to it, his face shadowed by the half-light of dawn. Celine froze, then turned to look at him with wide eyes. She didn't know if it was instinct or fate that told her who stood there, but when she realised it was Darius she broke into a run.

Her husband caught her as she threw herself at him, pressing his face into the side of her neck and whispering her name against her skin. Her hands roamed up his back, clinging to him.

'Cee—' he began, but Celine interrupted him as she slid her lips over his, swallowing the rest of his words with a kiss that shook her knees.

'Forgive me,' she huffed when their mouths parted, her eyes still wide with astonishment. 'I got scared, and I lashed out.'

'Celine…' The gentleness in his voice, along with the warmth radiating from his gaze, tore a sob from her throat when she saw nothing but forgiveness coming from him.

'I understand,' he whispered against her cheek, his lips brushing over her skin and causing a shiver to claw through her. 'I got upset, and I ran away again. *I* need to be the one to ask for forgiveness.'

Celine immediately shook her head and wrapped her arms around his torso to pull him closer. 'The week in São Paulo with you was the happiest I've ever been, but I was too scared to accept that, too tied up with everything here to see clearly.'

'But now you do?' he asked and when she nodded into his chest he pushed her away.

His hands came up to her face, cupping it from each side, his thumbs brushing over her cheeks. 'Then say yes—to *everything* this time. Say yes to us, our marriage, our family…our life together in São Paulo.'

His voice was deep and warm, her eyes fluttering closed as she imagined what their life would be like if she said yes. There he was, her missing piece, and she would never let go of him ever again.

'Yes.'

EPILOGUE

CELINE BREATHED IN the humidity surrounding her. The scent of the Amazon River mingling with the rainforest crept up her nose and gave her a strange longing. It had been a year since she'd left Santarém behind. She hadn't missed it, yet being back gave her a sense of nostalgia that pulled at her heart.

In the last year her life had developed in ways she couldn't have imagined. If anyone had told her that she would reconcile with her estranged husband after finally sending him divorce papers, she would have laughed in their face. But there he was, standing right next to her with his arm wrapped around her waist.

'Mirabel!' Nina shouted when she spotted her cousin. She glanced upwards, looking at her father, who nodded, and off she went to greet Mirabel.

Behind her they spotted Rafael, who waved at them as they picked their way through the gathering crowd. 'The dog show is becoming larger every year,' Celine said when they got close enough to hear each other, then she hugged her brother-in-law.

'I know. Maria says she's excited, but the amount of stress happening at home paints a different picture,' Rafael replied with a twinkle in his eyes, then he looked her up and down. 'You look well, Cee.'

Celine smiled, the genuine concern in her brother-in-law's expression warming her heart. 'So do you. I missed your face.'

'We miss you around here. Let me get Maria. She'll want to say hi before the show starts.' Rafael nodded towards Darius, then made his way to the judges' table, where Maria was setting up the scorecards.

Celine shivered when her husband's breath grazed over her cheek as he leaned into her. 'He has no idea, does he?' he asked, to which she huffed a laugh.

'Nope. But Maria will see it the second she spots me.' Nervous energy bubbled up within her.

After leaving to be with Darius in São Paulo, Celine had spent the first few weeks at home, getting herself and Nina settled into their new life. After reaching out to her old friends at the veterinary institute in Manaus, recruiters had started calling her, offering her partnerships at different practices or staff to start her own business. None of them had seemed right, until the offer she'd ended up accepting had landed in her inbox. Someone at the veterinary university in São Paulo had heard she'd moved there and offered her a teaching position. With Darius still working full-time as the head physician of Atlético Morumbi, the flexibility teaching at the university promised had been too good to pass up.

Plus, Professor Dr Dias-Delgado had a nice ring to it—though outside of Darius no one took the trouble to say her full title.

Since then they had another big change in their lives, one neither of them had expected.

'Oh, my God!' Maria knocked the wind out of her lungs when she threw herself at her sister in a tight hug. Next to her Celine heard Darius chuckle as he let go of her hand to give the sisters some space for their hug.

Maria planted both of her hands on her shoulders and pushed her away, looking her up and down. Then she turned her head and looked at Rafael with narrowed eyes. 'Why didn't you tell me she was pregnant?'

His eyes widened, then they dropped to her stomach that showed a small but clear bump.

'I…' he began, but Maria had already turned around to haul her into another hug.

'Why didn't *you* tell me?' she asked, the unbridled joy in her sister's eyes exactly the reaction she had wanted to see.

'I wanted to surprise you,' Celine replied, then reached out to pull Darius closer, his hand coming to rest on her stomach. 'We had another…accident, but as it turns out it was something we had both been thinking about.'

Darius moved his thumb over her stomach and smiled when their eyes met. 'This time we're doing it together—all the way.'

* * * * *